What if...

What if...

Two words. Endless possibilities.

What if...

On November 6, 2012, voters in Maine and Maryland approved ballot measures allowing same-sex marriage. In Washington State, after the legislature had passed and the governor had signed a law enacting same-sex marriage, opponents challenged it by placing the controversial issue on the ballot and subjecting it to a public vote. The challenge was defeated. In Minnesota, voters rejected a measure that would have banned same-sex marriage. Four states, the first to do so, approved same-sex marriage in a public vote on the same day. The timing was right. America was ready for a fundamental societal change. History was made.

For many people, especially those who had spent decades fighting for equal rights for gays, lesbians and bisexuals, this was a dream come true. To have the majority of voters support marriage equality for members of the LGB community was an important goal finally realized.

But, as followers of the Equal Rights Movement know, supportive public votes for their cause were rare, particularly the issue of same-sex marriage. In fact, in November 2004, eleven states voted on proposed state constitutional amendments banning same-sex marriage. All passed. The controversial issue had been placed on the ballots in those states to lure social conservatives to the polls and ensure Republican victories in many of the nation's close races. The divisive tactic worked, from the White House down to the state level.

However, the battle for same-sex marriage was not over. When the wedge issue was brought up again in 2012 by the right wing, the outcome was quite different. Voters in four states turned a wish, a hope, a fantasy into a dream come true for same-sex couples and gay rights activists across our nation. Two and a half years later, the US Supreme Court added an exclamation mark to that affirmation by ruling that the fundamental right to marry is guaranteed to same-sex couples by the Fourteenth Amendment.

The battle for equal rights, though, is not over. Other issues remain, housing and employment protections and transgender rights, for example. But a major victory, a long held dream, became reality in November 2012.

What if…

The issue of same-sex marriage, which is a part of the broader issue of gay rights, has been at the heart of a growing culture war that has divided the United States for years, decades. Progressives versus conservatives. The Left versus the Right. Blue states versus red states. Us versus them.

What if…

The United States was divided by a different culture war four decades before the November 2012 election. It was over the War in Vietnam. Doves versus Hawks. Antiwar activists versus the Establishment. "All we are saying is give peace a chance." versus "America: love it or leave it."

What if…

The angry words of the current culture war over gay issues have escalated over time. Charges. Counter-charges. Deceitful. Defensive. Inciting. Intentional. At what point does this war of words lead to destructive actions, violence, and eventually to civil war?

What if…

Radicals from the '70s gain power in this Twenty-First Century American civil war fought over gay rights and same-sex marriage. And they run it their way.

The Dark Blue Heart is set one year before the November 2012 election, before a quartet of states changed history. It is set in the fictitious state of Columbiana. But it could be Maine, Maryland, Washington, or Minnesota. Or Indiana or Colorado. It could be the state in which you live.

What if…

About the Author

Tom Nussbaum has written two other novels, *Completing the Course* and *The Boy in the Book,* and a memoir, *An "H" of a Life.* Born and raised in Seattle, Nussbaum graduated from the University of Washington. He was a high school special education teacher. He is retired and resides in Ajijic, Mexico where he is a member of the Ajijic Writers Group.

About *The Dark Blue Heart.*

"…this author has a lot of wisdom to pass on."

The Stranger, Seattle

"A breakneck novel at breakneck speed, *The Dark Blue Heart* is spawned from the oxygen of publicity conferred by TV breaking news. Conspicuously controversial.

Rosemary Grayson,
Former UK television newscaster,
Justice of the Peace

"Deftly told, with graphic scenes and clever use of the evening news to tell much of the story."

Jim Tipton,
Associate Editor *El Ojo del Lago,*
Author, poet, Colorado Book Award in Poetry winner

"…a good story about an alternate history in which both sides turn to violence and murder."

Mel Goldberg,
Retired college Creative Writing professor, author

THE DARK
BLUE HEART

THE DARK BLUE HEART

TOM NUSSBAUM

ISBN: 1530450284
ISBN 13: 9781530450282
Library of Congress Control Number: 2016904346
CreateSpace Independent Publishing Platform
North Charleston, South Carolina

*To the Ajijic Writers Group,
whose talented, wise members have taught and inspired me.*

PROLOGUE

VALENTINE'S DAY, 2011

A giant pink plastic cupid straddles the gaping entryway of the former warehouse. To the left, a red-lettered poster announces: "Red B4 Bed Party Feb. 14." To the right, a sign declares: "'Wear Red,' Cupid Said." Slapped on the sign at a forty-five degree angle, a pink patch specifies "10 p.m.-2 a.m."

A muscular bouncer wearing a red jock strap and a tight red tank top stands guard. A ramp zigzags to the entrance from a gravel parking lot below. The bouncer lets in one-by-one and, more appropriately on Valentine's Day, two-by-two the growing line of red-clad partygoers who snake up the ramp.

The warehouse is now a popular gay bar, a dance club, called Snakes. The name has little to do with the manner in which the people line up on the ramp.

As music throbs within the club and seeps through its doors and windows into the shadowy night, two young men lean against the building catching their breath. They had been dancing and they are wet with sweat. One wears red boxers covered in small white hearts. The other is in a red Speedo, his torso sprinkled with red glitter. He fans himself with caution, avoiding glittered areas. Two young women burst through the club's wide doorway. They are wearing matching red T-shirts and jeans. The bigger, butch woman, who is wearing a red St. Louis Cardinals baseball cap backward, has the smaller, boyish one by the elbow and steers her like a shopping cart with a faulty fourth wheel through the red-garbed queue. They make it to the bottom of the ramp and into the lot where between two parked cars the smaller woman doubles over and vomits on the gravel, her eruption covering the side of a Goodyear tire.

"Babe," the bigger woman says as she doffs her cap and begins fanning her partner, "I'm taking you home."

"No," whines the incapacitated woman, "the governor signed…"

"I know, babe. But you're sick. You've had too much to drink. We need to go home. I'll make you some tea."

"No," the drunk lesbian repeats with an inebriated slur. She pauses. A delayed reaction. "Tea? Can I have peppermint?"

"If that's what you want."

"Oh. OK." She stands up and steadies herself on her partner's forearm. "I don't feel good, Syd."

"I know, babe."

Two older men step out of the club. One appears to be in his early fifties. He is wearing white shorts, the kind one wears to an exclusive, proper croquet party, and a white shirt. He has accessorized them with red suspenders and knee-high red socks. His white tennis shoes have red laces. The other man looks to be at least a decade older, somewhat heavier, and sporting bright red silk pajamas. Each wears a blue and yellow Human Rights Campaign equal sign button on his top's left pocket. The buttons stand out in the sea of crimson like blue and yellow pansies in a field of red tulips.

"I'm too old for this," the pajama-clad man says. "I didn't recognize any of the music. Couldn't they have played one song from the '70s?"

"Couldn't they have turned the volume down?" snaps the other man. "OK. We've celebrated the signing of the law. Can we go home now?"

"Yes," the older man answers. But the one-syllable answer is cut short. He suddenly begins to cry. "I still can't believe the legislature passed and the governor signed a gay marriage law today. In Columbiana. In my lifetime. Oh, my god!" The man buries his head into his partner's chest and begins to sob so hard he no longer can talk. The younger man holds him, caressing the back of his head.

A stunning, statuesque woman exits the door, stops, and takes a breath of cool night air. She is garbed in a crimson mini-skirt, matching lace bra, and jet black stiletto heels. Blood red lipstick covers her lips as if they were hand painted raspberries. Her detailed makeup appears to have been applied by a professional cosmetician. Her perfectly coiffed curly red hair frames her face and cascades around her shoulders. She is followed by a man who is taller than she is. He exudes ethnic mystery and startling handsomeness. He is wearing red Levis and bowtie. He has no shirt and is barefoot. They look like models on a photo shoot.

"Shane stopped in the can. He'll be out in a minute," the man says in a calm voice. Then without pausing, his tone changes. "OMG, girl, I am so fucked up!" They walk with careful, delicate steps down the ramp, desperately trying to maintain their balance and dignity. They teeter toward a nearby blue Dumpster. The man pulls a pack of cigarettes from a back pocket and hands the woman a cigarette. As he lights it, a thunderous explosion from within the dance club shatters the moment. The force of the blast shoves the couple forward onto the gravel. Debris rains around them.

"What the hell?" the woman asks as the man inquires perfunctorily if she is OK. Neither question is answered. The man and woman are each focused on his or her own condition. Realizing they are uninjured, the startled duo gets up and staggers away from the building. Around them, shrieking and yelling competes with the electronic dance rhythms from inside. People begin pouring out the doorway within seconds. Suddenly, the music stops and only the sounds of panic can be heard: shrieks, screams, moans, coughs, cries, frantic voices shouting names.

"Where's Shane? Shane!" the man says much louder than he realizes. "Shane!" he calls again as two poorly made-up drag queens in matching inexpensive red cocktail dresses race past him screaming at each other in a foreign language. Neither the man nor the woman notices them. "Shane!" the woman shouts, fear and desperation wrestling in her voice, as they step closer to Snakes scanning the frantic, fleeing crowd.

2011

January

S	M	T	W	T	F	S
						1
2	3	4	5	6	7	8
9	10	11	12	13	14	15
16	17	18	19	20	21	22
23	24	25	26	27	28	29
30	31					

February

S	M	T	W	T	F	S
		1	2	3	4	5
6	7	8	9	10	11	12
13	14	15	16	17	18	19
20	21	22	23	24	25	26
27	28					

March

S	M	T	W	T	F	S
		1	2	3	4	5
6	7	8	9	10	11	12
13	14	15	16	17	18	19
20	21	22	23	24	25	26
27	28	29	30	31		

April

S	M	T	W	T	F	S
					1	2
3	4	5	6	7	8	9
10	11	12	13	14	15	16
17	18	19	20	21	22	23
24	25	26	27	28	29	30

May

S	M	T	W	T	F	S
1	2	3	4	5	6	7
8	9	10	11	12	13	14
15	16	17	18	19	20	21
22	23	24	25	26	27	28
29	30	31				

June

S	M	T	W	T	F	S
			1	2	3	4
5	6	7	8	9	10	11
12	13	14	15	16	17	18
19	20	21	22	23	24	25
26	27	28	29	30		

July

S	M	T	W	T	F	S
					1	2
3	4	5	6	7	8	9
10	11	12	13	14	15	16
17	18	19	20	21	22	23
24	25	26	27	28	29	30
31						

August

S	M	T	W	T	F	S
	1	2	3	4	5	6
7	8	9	10	11	12	13
14	15	16	17	18	19	20
21	22	23	24	25	26	27
28	29	30	31			

September

S	M	T	W	T	F	S
				1	2	3
4	5	6	7	8	9	10
11	12	13	14	15	16	17
18	19	20	21	22	23	24
25	26	27	28	29	30	

October

S	M	T	W	T	F	S
						1
2	3	4	5	6	7	8
9	10	11	12	13	14	15
16	17	18	19	20	21	22
23	24	25	26	27	28	29
30	31					

November

S	M	T	W	T	F	S
		1	2	3	4	5
6	7	8	9	10	11	12
13	14	15	16	17	18	19
20	21	22	23	24	25	26
27	28	29	30			

December

S	M	T	W	T	F	S
				1	2	3
4	5	6	7	8	9	10
11	12	13	14	15	16	17
18	19	20	21	22	23	24
25	26	27	28	29	30	31

WEDNESDAY, FEBRUARY 2, 2011

Columbiana City's Number One News Source--KEHT Channel 8--February 2, 2011 crawled across the bottom of the television screen. "And in Stover today," a news anchorman's deep voice filled the disheveled living room, "the state senate passed the controversial gay marriage bill by a vote of 25 to 20. Coupled with last week's house passage of the bill, the long-fought legislation will go to Governor Kristoff Oleson who has said he will sign it on February 14, Valentine's Day, only twelve days away. The law will go into effect January 1, 2012."

Cary Foreman watched the newscast from his cozy, gray Lazy-Boy recliner. He sat slumped in the decades-old chair, exhausted from the stresses of the day and beaten by all the battles he had fought over the years. Next to him, a tarnished lamp with a discolored lampshade stood on a tired end table covered with stacks of books and magazines. Atop the piles, implying they had been perused recently, were a yellowed, crinkly copy of *Jonathan Livingston Seagull*, a *Rolling Stone* featuring an article on "The Protest Songs of the '60s and '70s," and an issue of *Car*, a British magazine, featuring a history of American compact cars. The lamp's soft illumination bathed the overloaded table and cluttered room in late-night sleepiness.

Although fatigued, Cary's posture tensed upon hearing the announcement about the gay marriage bill. He sat up just a bit and slammed his right fist onto the tattered armrest. "At last," he whispered. "Now the real war can finally begin." He paused a beat and added, "It's always been inevitable." Then, as if an afterthought, he gazed heavenward. He took a slow, deep breath, smiled with a mix of satisfaction and disbelief, and grabbed the remote control. The television screen went dark.

THURSDAY, FEBRUARY 3, 2011

Dashing into his unkempt living room the next night, Cary knew KEHT's *The 11 O'Clock News* was about to begin. He had come home later than normal, the result of a hectic, problem-ridden work day. But he wanted to see how the media reported the hastily scheduled press conference triggered by the prior day's legislative action. Still wearing his navy blue North Face winter coat, he sank into his recliner, even more tired than he had been the night before, and leaned back. He picked up the remote from the shabby end table and clicked.

KEHT Channel 8--February 3, 2011 crawled across the bottom of the screen as the image of a lean, taut-lipped man angrily addressing a row of microphones adorned with call letters, channel numbers, and logos. The crawl ended and was replaced by a stationary caption identifying the speaker as Rev. Al Kirk, a minister and gay marriage opponent.

"If the governor signs this abomination on February 14 as he has promised, we will begin collecting signatures to have the issue of homosexual marriage put to a public vote in November," Kirk challenged. "Let there be no mistake about this: if Governor Oleson signs this legislation, a law passed by an amoral legislature, an elected body completely out of touch with its constituents' values, he has declared war on all Columbianans, not just those here in Columbiana City, who value family, freedom, and the Bible. He has, in fact, declared war on decent Americans all across the United States. What is happening here in Columbiana could happen in any state. But, apparently, God has chosen us to stand up to and defend against the opening salvo in this war. And we shall." Kirk, staring into KEHT's camera, shook his fist. "This has become a culture war between those who live in a culture of decency and those who promote a culture of sin. We will fight this war all the way to the ballot box."

"OK. It's on," Cary mumbled. His tired eyelids fluttered like the wings of a dying butterfly. *Al Kirk said it all,* Cary thought as he struggled to upright himself. *He's inspired me. But I can't deal with this right now. I have got to go to bed.*

The video ended. A reporter, a pleasant-faced, middle-aged woman, appeared, KEHT on her microphone, and spoke to the camera. But the exhausted man in the recliner did not hear her, for as soon as she appeared, he shut off the TV, dropping the remote to the floor in the same motion. In an instant, he was asleep.

FRIDAY, FEBRUARY 4, 2011

By the time the gray-haired, pony-tailed man reached the head of the Starbuck's line, he had forgotten what he wanted to order. It was a simple old-fashioned coffee. He remembered that. But he couldn't recall how to order it in the new Starbuck lingo. The barista greeted him and smiled.

"I'll have, um, coffee, regular coffee," the man stammered.

"What size?"

"Oh, um, vente? Grande?" His confused gaze darted to the list of drinks on the wall. "Whichever is medium?"

"Room for cream?"

"No. Black, please." His order completed, he exhaled with relief.

The barista spun around, poured the coffee from a carafe on the counter behind him. "You don't come in here often, do you?" he asked the man as he handed him his coffee.

"No. Not really. I just want plain old coffee. Like I have for forty years. Too many choices today." And then the man released a deep laugh, a laugh that somehow combined jolly with sinister.

At a nearby table, Cary looked up from his laptop. He turned and leaned his bald head toward the laughter as if searching for its source. Finding it quickly, his face reacted in a mix of confusion, recognition, and disbelief. He watched as the pony-tailed man headed in his direction toward an empty table near him.

"Kayo?" he asked as the man passed. The man looked down at the questioning voice. He waited a moment to answer, to allow time to assess the question's source.

"Yes?"

"Oh, my god. Kayo? It's you. I'd know that laugh anywhere. Even after, I don't know, thirty-five years."

It was then Kayo's turn to recognize, to react. "Cary? Oh, no way. Cary Foreman. I don't believe it. Is that you? How are you, man?" But before Cary could reply, he was standing and the two men were hugging. Kayo's coffee sloshed.

As they separated and stared at each other, Cary sputtered, "Holy shit! Look at you. You haven't changed a bit. You still have a pony tail." At the same moment, Kayo said, without hearing Cary's words, "Wait! Where's your hair?" And then, as if he had been performing it for decades with a touring cast of *Hair*, he belted "Give me a head with hair, long beautiful hair, shining, streaming…" Kayo sort of snorted the last word as be burst into his recognizable laugh. Cary joined him.

The other Starbuck's patrons looked up irritated, briefly ending conversations or ceasing their typing and screen staring.

"The hair is gone, man," Cary answered unnecessarily. He motioned to a chair at his table. "Sit."

As both men sat, Cary said, "The last time I saw you, man, was while you were…" He paused.

"…in prison," Kayo finished the sentence. "And I told you not to come back, not to incriminate yourself. That we'd catch up later. But thirty-five years later?"

"And I moved to Kauai right after that. Disappeared. Had to. Your getting locked up after all we'd been through together. It was just too close. I was scared."

"And rightfully so. I don't blame you. Never did," Kayo said. "So, how are you, man? What are you doing? Where has life taken you?"

"Oh, where to begin? Went to Hawaii. Spent a lot of time laying low. Was with Joyce until she died. Cancer. One kid, a son. He's still there. Took some classes. Eventually got a degree."

For twenty minutes, Cary and Kayo caught up, ricocheting through past memories and the last three-plus decades in disjointed sentences, incomplete thoughts, and omitted details. Kayo, in particular, omitted details. Intentionally. The old friends sipped coffee. They exchanged email addresses and phone numbers. Suddenly, Cary looked at his watch. "Man, I gotta go. I gotta class to teach."

"You teach?"

"Yeah. History. At MetComm."

"You teach at Metropolitan Community College?" Kayo muttered with surprise.

Cary stood. "Man, running into you has just made my day. What a rush!" He paused and looked Kayo in the eyes. "We'll be in touch. And it won't be in thirty-five years." He patted Kayo on the shoulder and raced past him toward the coffeehouse door, a broad smile of contentment on his face. A familiar, unique laugh followed him onto the street.

TUESDAY, FEBRUARY 15, 2011

KEHT Channel 8--February 15, 2011--2 Dead in Gay Bar Explosion announced the ticker as it crept across the television screen as thirtyish morning news anchor Lacey Powers welcomed her viewers. Her makeup was too stark, her hair too teased and sprayed for a beauty pageant let alone the early morning.

"It is 6:01 and we begin the news with the shocking report of a fatal explosion at Snakes, a local gay dance club. Kimberly Teller is at the scene. Good morning, Kimberly. What can you tell us?"

"Good morning, Lacey," the middle-aged reporter replied from the scene. Kimberly Teller's makeup was less showy, more natural. Behind her, Snakes' partially blown-out wall formed an ideal story-telling backdrop. Remnants of a red-lettered banner danced in the light morning breeze behind the reporter. "The explosion took place at 11:58 last night. The crowded club, Snakes, was celebrating Valentine's Day and the signing earlier yesterday of the gay marriage bill by Governor Kristoff Oleson. Two fatalities are confirmed and ten people are hospitalized. Their condition is unknown. At least another dozen partygoers sustained minor injuries and were treated at the scene and released."

"Do we know what caused the explosion, Kimberly?" the anchor asked.

"Not for certain. But we know it took place in a men's bathroom. That is where the deaths and most serious injuries occurred. Club manager Trace Stevens told me it appears to have been caused by a bomb. But that has not been confirmed. Investigators are expected momentarily."

"Do the police have any suspects?"

"I have Officer Patrick Kovach with me," Kimberly said as the camera panned out, bringing the policeman into the picture. "Are there any suspects?" the reporter asked the tall, stone-faced officer.

"Well, we haven't determined the cause. But we are following some leads and urge any witnesses who have not spoken to police to come forward. The smallest bit of information may be the most important piece in determining what happened and apprehending those responsible if, in fact, it was intentional."

"OK, Lacey. That is all we know at this point. As I said, investigators are expected shortly and we await identification of the victims as soon as families have been notified. We will have more information on the Noon News. Back to you, Lacey."

Cary stared at the screen from his Lazy-Boy recliner, his eyes wide open, his jaw hanging in disbelief. "Oh, my god," he said in shock. "Just as I predicted."

He had had a restless night. A mysterious, inner excitement kept quality sleep at bay. He had semi-slept in spurts since eleven-thirty, but had given up at 5:53 a.m., just in time for the morning news. Now, with the upsetting report fresh in his ears, he returned to bed, pulled the covers over his head, and hoped to doze off and escape the real world. He managed, oddly enough, to sleep for more than an hour and wake up well-rested. But, once up, the disturbing news of the explosion and subsequent deaths haunted him through the morning. He puttered in an unfocused manner until he sat down to watch the Noon News and learn of any developments.

Columbiana City's Number One News Source--KEHT Channel 8--Feb. 15, 2011 crawled across the bottom of the television screen. Lacey Powers appeared with co-anchor, Mac Hines, a fifty-something African American.

"We lead off with new information regarding last night's fatal explosion at gay dance club Snakes," Mac said. "Kimberly Teller reports from the scene. Good afternoon, Kimberly."

"Good afternoon, Mac and Lacey. We now know the names of the two fatalities. We also have confirmation that the explosion was caused by a bomb," announced Kimberly. "The victims are 22-year-old Shane Collier of Columbiana City and 34-year-old Marty Beck of Linnton. Two unidentified men remain in Metropolitan Hospital in critical condition. Six others are in serious condition and two men with lesser injuries were released this morning."

"What details can you tell us about the bomb and do the police have any suspects?" asked Lacey.

"Police believe the bomb was a homemade device and was placed in or under a toilet. The injured and dead were either in the bathroom or just outside its door. I was told by witnesses that shattered porcelain and wood and splattered blood and body parts were scattered throughout the restroom."

"That is shocking, Kimberly. Do the police have any leads?" Lacey pressed.

"They haven't said. But they did tell me a number of witnesses have come forward and provided vital information." As Kimberly said that, the camera pulled back revealing a young man with tired eyes, mussed hair, a navy blue sweat shirt, and remnants of red glitter on his cheeks and hair. "This is Kurt Lampman. He was at Snakes last night. Can you tell us what you saw?"

"Well, I had just stepped outside to cool off. And 'Boom!' it just went off," Kurt began. "I felt the blast and saw the wall," he pointed toward the blast site, "sort of buckle and debris fall all around. There was a lot of panicked screaming and people were running everywhere. It was chaos. Immediate chaos."

"But," Kimberly interrupted, "as you told me earlier, you saw something that caught your eye."

"Yes. And it is so weird I noticed it in the commotion. But I did. These two ugly drag queens wearing really tacky red party dresses, like from K-Mart, burst through the crowd and began running to the end of the block," he elaborated. "What I first noticed was that they were yelling at each other. It was controlled yelling. Not freaked-out shrieking. And they were yelling in what I think was Russian. It might have been some other East European language, but it was definitely not English. And they had on tennis shoes, running shoes, not heels. Why I noticed that, I'm not sure. But everyone knows you don't wear flats with a red party dress!"

"Well," Kimberly said with a twitch of a smile, "that may be an important detail. Thank you, Kurt." She turned to the camera. "I hope to have more interviews with witnesses and police investigators on *The News @ 5*. Back to you at the studio."

"We understand the FBI is getting involved in the investigation," Mac said, addressing the audience. "Was this a hate crime? We'll find out more at five."

Russians Seen Running from Gay Bar Blast read the brief headline creeping across the bottom of television screens across Columbiana as *The News @ 5* began. Cary, however, was not watching the news. He was at MetComm, preparing for an evening class. Mac Hines immediately threw to Kimberly Teller who was again standing in front of Snakes.

"The FBI is calling this a hate crime," Kimberly said. "Earlier today, I interviewed a witness who noticed two men speaking Russian or an Eastern European language running from the club. A few hours later, police announced a second witness had corroborated that account."

"Who was this witness, Kimberly?"

"He is a 42-year-old man, Mac. He was on foot, nearing Snakes, when he heard the blast. He sped up to see what had happened when two men in red dresses ran in front of him yelling in Russian."

"Does this man understand Russian, Kimberly?"

"Yes. He studied it after the fall of the Berlin Wall. He says they were shouting 'Hurry!' and 'Move!' As they reached the end of the parking lot, where it meets the street, the headlights of a dark-colored car suddenly beamed, blinding the witness. According to this second witness, the men hopped in the car yelling 'Let's go!' in Russian. The car raced away before the doors were even slammed.

"Kimberly, did this man see the car's license plate?"

"No. He couldn't see the front license plate because of the bright headlights. It was then he noticed the commotion at Snakes and didn't think to look at the back plate."

"Did the club have any security cameras?" Mac asked.

"Only outside, over the entrance. The ones inside were being replaced, upgraded. They were to be reconnected in mid-week. But, obviously, that would be too late to help with this investigation," Kimberly explained. "Back to you, Mac."

Nothing new was added to Kimberly's report for *The 11 O'Clock News*. But Cary, just home from campus, watched the rehash of the earlier reports from his recliner. He was puzzled and fascinated by what he heard. *Who are these guys? Are they working with Al Kirk or independently?* He scratched his bald head just behind his right ear. *I need to find them.*

WEDNESDAY, FEBRUARY 16, 2011

"It's Cary. I hope it's not too late to call."

"Hey, man. I was just thinking about you. And our conversation. And running into you like that. No. It's not too late. It's not even ten," Kayo replied.

"Yeah. It really was great seeing you at Starbuck's, man. I meant to call earlier, but I have this weird work schedule. I teach three classes between one o'clock and eight. Since one of the classes is in the evening, I'm sometimes still at school well after eight. Frequently, actually."

"That sounds like it makes for a long day," Kayo said. "A tiring one, too."

"It does," Cary replied. "So, since I have mornings free, I usually take care of personal business then or after I get home."

"I'm still processing that you became a teacher, man. A college professor, no less." Kayo chuckled a quiet version of his unique laugh.

"Anyway," Cary continued, "I'd like to continue our conversation. We got more to talk about. Unfinished business. Can we have coffee again tomorrow? Same place. A little earlier?"

"Sure," Kayo answered. "I'd like that. And you're right. We do have unfinished business."

THURSDAY, FEBRUARY 17, 2011

Cary was seated at a corner table sipping his coffee when Kayo strolled into the Starbuck's. He watched Kayo order his "regular coffee, grande, medium," and then twist between several chairs to the corner table.

"It is so good to see you again, man. So good," Cary greeted his old friend as he reached the table. Kayo sat down, his back to the open room forming a shield from prying eyes and eavesdropping ears.

"I know, Cary. I feel like we've gone back in time. Like we're back there, back then again."

"Exactly. What a perfect segue. I got a question for you," Cary said as soon as Kayo was settled. "And I know it is out of left field, but," and he waited a beat, "do you miss the old times? Do you miss what we used to do?"

Kayo released a short chuckle. "Yeah. In a way. Yeah. I do." He paused. "You know, man, I don't think I've ever actually said that. You'd think I'd have learned my lesson. But, yes, I do miss it. I have to admit, every once in a while I wonder what it would be like to cause a little turmoil and give my adrenaline a reason to flow again like it did during that damn Vietnam War." Kayo paused again. "Yeah. I guess I still have the need to raise hell. Raisin' hell? Wasn't that what we called what we were doing? Not protesting. Not demonstrating. Not engaging in violence. None of the terms the media used. Just raisin' hell." Kayo gazed into the distance, embraced by nostalgia for a moment. He quickly shook his head and returned to the present. "Man, I haven't done anything like that in a long time. Haven't found a reason, a cause. But I've wanted to, I guess."

"Haven't found a reason? Haven't found a cause?" Cary reacted with disbelief. "The environment? Our fucking up Iraq? The corporate takeover of our elections? The Tea Party and the racist way it treats Obama? A fucked-up tax system? 'Don't Ask, Don't Tell'? Haven't found a cause?" Cary stopped and exhaled his agitation and frustration, calmed down, and took a cautious breath. "You didn't even join Act Up?" he asked, curiosity permeating the question.

"What?" Kayo responded sharply. "Act Up? Why are you asking that?"

"Because Act Up's disruptive tactics were the closest thing to those of the anti-war protesters. And, I assume, it was focused on something you could relate to: Stopping AIDS and fighting for funding to find a cure." His tone was now controlled and nonjudgmental. "You are gay, aren't you?"

"And why the hell are you asking *that*?" Kayo asked. He peeked over his shoulder to see if anyone was close enough to hear.

"Because I have to. Because I always thought you were. Because when you got released, you disappeared. None of the old gang knew where you were. I thought you finally figured it all out, you found your way. I assumed you joined a gay community somewhere. I even worried you had died of AIDS."

"You thought I was gay? Why? How?" But before Cary could answer, Kayo replied to the earlier question. "Yes. I'm gay, Cary. But I didn't even know in the '70s. How did you?"

"Man, I hate to tell you, but there were times when we got stoned that you gave yourself away, you let your guard down."

"I did? My guard? I didn't have a guard. I didn't know," Kayo snapped. "When?"

"Like when Ben Lieber was around."

Kayo's tense posture suddenly relaxed. His face instantaneously softened, morphing into an adolescent's expression experiencing first love.

"Oh, my god, man," Cary reacted. "You should see yourself right now. That is the look you had whenever Ben was around. It hasn't changed. Even after thirty-five years. You were in love with Ben. We all knew that."

"No, I wasn't. I admired him. I thought he was really smart. And cool."

"And you were in love with him," Cary added.

The friends sat in silence looking at each other for a few seconds. "OK. Maybe I was," Kayo conceded. "But I didn't even realize it or understand it. Maybe I didn't have enough time to deal with my feelings because I was so focused and involved in our work. But you figured it out before I did?"

"Apparently."

"That's funny," Kayo said. He released a brief spurt of his jolly, but sinister laugh. Then he snapped back to his original posture and facial expression. He shook his head. "No. This is awkward, man. Foreign territory. I'm not comfortable with this conversation. For the record, this sort of stuff, feelings, talking about being gay, is not something I share with people."

"For the record," Cary echoed with a tinge of sarcasm, "I am not 'people.' This is me, man, Cary Foreman, you're talking to. And why don't you talk about this sort of stuff? It is the twenty-first century. The world has changed. It's OK."

"I know that. I know that intellectually, Cary. But you didn't go through what I did. You didn't get caught. You didn't go to prison. You didn't live in a world where you kept every feeling, every emotion inside. You could not let anyone know what you were feeling. It would be exploited; you'd be victimized. There were times, man, when I stuffed everything down so deep inside even I didn't know what I was really thinking or feeling." Kayo's hands began shaking and he set down his cup. He tried to calm himself with a long, slow breath. "You don't know, man. You can't know," his voice trembled. He sighed again and wiggled his fingers in an attempt to rid the shaking. "OK. You want to hear the story, the real story?"

"Of course I do, Kayo. I've always wanted to know what happened to you. Yes, I want to hear your story. We've shared too much for me not to want to," he said, as he sat back.

"You may have suspected I was gay back then, Cary, but I didn't know. How could I know for sure? I never discussed it. I hadn't acted on it. And it was never mentioned in the media back then. I had no information, no support. But within a week of being incarcerated, I was forced to suck off this biker guy who was in for murder. You know, the new piece of meat sort of thing. Teach him who's in charge. Well, to my surprise, giving this guy a blow job came natural to me and I enjoyed it," he said sheepishly. "But, of course, I couldn't let on that I enjoyed it. And I immediately realized I had to keep my distance from this guy before he made me his property and expected more from me than blow jobs. And I was not ready to go beyond blow jobs. Especially with him. Well, unbelievably, two nights later, he was killed by a drug dealer and there was a shake-up at the prison. Among other changes, I was moved to another site, one housing what appeared to be less dangerous people. I'm not sure why I was selected, but I'm glad I was. And I was never sexually exploited in the new prison."

Kayo stopped, sipped his coffee. "About two years later, a guy named Dan arrived. The first thing I noticed about him was he was really handsome. At first, I avoided him because he made me uncomfortable. It was, I know now, because I couldn't deal with my attraction to him, my feelings. This was something I had tried to ignore, hide from for years. Well, eventually, we did meet and immediately learned we were jailed for almost identical reasons. He had bombed an army recruitment office, seriously injuring a recruiter, a guy named Sgt. James Balfour, who was sleeping in a back room. It was night and Dan had no idea anyone was in the office. Dan had no intention of hurting anyone and, as a result, felt incredible guilt and remorse. He had recurring nightmares about Balfour. Did you ever have nightmares about the bombing, Cary?"

"No. Not really. All we did was bomb the university ROTC building, totaling a bunch of military property and setting fire to a ton of records." Cary smiled. "It wasn't all peace, love, harmony, and tolerance back then, was it?"

"Hell, no," Kayo responded to the rhetorical question. His answer was accompanied by a hint of his recognizable laugh. "We were the doves back then, the peacemakers. How ironic! We bombed buildings. They were the hawks, the warmongers. But they didn't bomb our buildings. We were more aligned with the Democrats, which today would be associated with the color blue, and they were more aligned with Republicans, which today means red. But they used blue-clad cops to bash our heads with Billy clubs at protests. And that made our heads red with blood. Again, how ironic. Think about this: if we were philosophically connected to Democrats, man, at our core we were quite a dark blue." Kayo paused.

The pair sat in silence for a moment. Cary suddenly sat up and smiled. "Do you remember the fight between Mike Dougherty and Chip…Chip…What the hell was Chip's last name? I can see him in front of me."

"Oh, my god! Cary, I haven't thought about that in decades," Kayo laughed. "What was that fight about anyway? I can just picture them pushing and shoving each other, but I don't remember why."

"One of them wanted to enter the freeway on an exit ramp and block the exiting traffic. The other insisted we enter on the entrance ramp because that was what it was for. As if we were about following rules." Kayo started to snort his signature laugh.

Cary leaned forward, placed his forehead on the table and cackled into it. "They almost came to blows," he sputtered.

"Well, didn't Chip have Mike pushed up against the wall?"

"And didn't Mike have his hands around Chip's neck?" Cary countered.

"Yes," Kayo answered. "But in a peace, love, and harmony sort of way."

Cary laughed so hard he made wheezing noises. He slapped the table with an open palm. Kayo released a final signature chortle, grabbed a paper napkin from the dispenser on the table and dabbed his eyes.

His composure regained, Kayo returned to the story of his life. "Anyway," he said, "Dan and I became friends, support systems, and somehow our relationship evolved into love. We didn't think of it as 'gay' love; it was just love. But, obviously, we couldn't let anyone around us know that and we certainly couldn't act on it often or openly. While it was frustrating as all hell, it was what kept us going, kept us sane. Five years later, I was released. I moved to Braxton, had my own apartment, farmed a bit, and worked part-time as a portrait photographer." Kayo paused a moment and stared over Cary's shoulder at a painting of an enormous coffee bean engulfed in flames. "Interesting painting," he noted. Cary, focused on Kayo's story, did not look. "Dan was released a year after me," Kayo continued. "With a little legal maneuvering, he was able to move in with me soon after he was released. Like I said, Dan had a lot of nightmares. 'Guiltmares,' he called them. Sometimes they were of the actual explosion. Sometimes they were of Balfour screaming in pain. Sometimes they were of Balfour staring at Dan from his wheelchair in court. Sometimes they were of Balfour's beautiful, blonde, angelic wife, Grace, sobbing on the witness stand testifying about her husband's injuries and suffering. Anyway, Dan and I were together until 1993 when he died in a car wreck. I moved to Stover a year after Dan died. Couldn't stay in Braxton. Not with the memories. Besides, I didn't have any friends there. We didn't have any real friends, straight or gay. I ran a small photography studio in Stover. And then I moved back here about a year ago. On a whim. Felt it was time to come home."

"Sort of back to the scene of the crime," Cary chuckled.

"Yeah. I guess. I didn't really belong in Stover. I had no connection to it and I didn't develop any connections in it. I was alone. Worse than that, Cary, was that I couldn't figure out where I did belong." Kayo looked down at the table. "Columbiana City sort of won by default," he continued, looking up. "Maybe, I thought, it was time to come back."

"Well, I'm glad you're here, man," Cary said.

"I'm not sure I'm going to stay. But I've been here a year and I haven't left. I keep thinking I'm supposed to find my purpose here."

Cary stared, processing Kayo's last statement. *How perfect,* he thought. *He just gave me the perfect lead-in I need to ask him to…No. The timing isn't right. Not yet.* Cary shook his head. He searched for something to say, something appropriate, something that would not betray his thoughts. "I can't believe you lived in Braxton.

It's such a conservative little town in the middle of nowhere," he mumbled, sidestepping the more serious issues and avoiding the more delicate questions.

"We kept to ourselves there," Kayo continued. "We were private. We had learned to be in prison. That is why I was so stunned when you asked if I were gay and involved in Act Up. Even though Dan and I had been anti-government rebels raisin' hell in our younger days, we had left all that behind. We were not a part of any activism, gay or otherwise. We had learned to be protective. Besides, Dan and I joked that Act Up was too tame, too civil. Fruit pies in the face and flour bombs were funny, not threatening. They needed to take a lesson from our anti-Vietnam War handbook in their disruptions. They needed to grow a pair."

Kayo stopped. He briefly looked at the flaming coffee bean painting again. "Well that's it, man. That's my life. That's my big secret, the secret I have kept from everyone from the past, the secret I kept from you." He paused again. "What do you think? Any questions or comments?" Then he laughed. This time the sound that mixed jolly with sinister somehow included nervousness. He gazed down at his coffee, avoiding his friend's eyes.

"Look," Cary said after a short pause, "I don't know what to say except, it's OK. You're OK. You and me, we're OK. That doesn't change anything, man. We were brothers against the war. We were brothers against the government. We're brothers now." He reached across the table and took Kayo's hand. Kayo looked down at the two hands and then up into Cary's eyes. "Are we good, man?" Cary asked.

"Yes." Kayo answered as his long-held fears and pent-up tension evaporated. An internal calm took over. The conversation he had dreaded for decades had ended with Cary holding his hand. *This is better than I ever dreamed,* he thought. Simultaneously, they squeezed each other's hand.

"Well, then," Cary continued, "that leads me to my next point, the reason I called you, the reason I wanted to meet with you." He let go of Kayo's hand and sat up a bit. "You told me you miss the old times. You said you think you're supposed to find your purpose here. But you said you hadn't been involved in activism since the '70s because you hadn't found a reason, a cause. Right?"

"Yes. I don't have anything I feel strong enough about to fight for or to risk everything for. It's been so long, I don't know if I would even remember how to do the kind of shit we did in the '70s."

Cary stared at Kayo. "I think you'd know how, man. And, more importantly, I think you know what you need to fight for. That's why you're here. I have a proposition for you, my friend."

"You do? What?"

"Not to be discussed here. But you know where. Ten o'clock Sunday morning," Cary winked. "I know you'll be there. By the way, Kayo," Cary paused, "this is the last time we can be seen in public together for a while." Then Cary stood up, smiled at Kayo and walked out of Starbuck's into bright February sunlight.

FRIDAY, FEBRUARY 18, 2011

The vision of a 1970s newspaper headline startled Cary out of a restless sleep: *Kayo'd: Radical Found Guilty.* He stared at the ceiling. *Was that in the Columbiana City Chronicle or the University of Columbiana Columns?* he tried to remember. *Wait. That was a dream. The masthead said the Hanoi Herald. Why was I dreaming about the Hanoi Herald? Is there a Hanoi Herald? Why was it in English? Oh my god. It was just a dream!* Cary felt his heart racing and heard his heavy breathing.

It was several clock ticks past dawn. Cary's room was blanketed in gray, two or three shades lighter than night. Agitated and restless, Cary remained in bed, wide-eyed, gazing at the ceiling. He was thinking about the past he had shared with Kayo, reflecting on his own history, and recalling the details of Kayo's childhood they'd discussed over a joint one long-ago afternoon.

Cary remembered Kayo's tale of how he got his unusual name. He was born Kirk Oswald Alexander on October 8, 1952, to Henry and Eva Alexander. Henry, Hank to his friends, was a college art history professor whose love for the visual arts instilled in his son a curiosity and appreciation for photography. Hank had served in World War II, had received a life-altering leg injury, and, as a result, had a noticeable limp. Kirk's mother, a French war bride, had been Hank's nurse during the post-surgery stage of his recovery. They developed a close relationship and maintained a letter-writing relationship after Hank was shipped stateside. Their love survived the miles and years of separation and Eva eventually followed him to the U.S. in 1949.

Three years later, Kirk was born. He was named after one of his father's war buddies, Ozzie Kirkendahl. Kirkendahl had been killed in action in the same battle that had so seriously injured Hank. Ozzie Kirkendahl's name morphed into Kirk Oswald – or Kayo as he was called within minutes of arriving home from the hospital. As a youngster, Kayo liked being named after "a war hero," as Hank referred to Ozzie.

As a fair-haired and even fairer complexioned young boy, Kirk was proud of his father's role in the military and war. By the time he entered junior high school, however, Kirk had grown to resent how his father's war injuries limited him from participating in many father-son activities. He was angry when he saw his father struggle with things others easily managed and took for granted, like putting on matching, normal-sized shoes or climbing stairs. "It isn't fair," Kirk often complained as he watched his father patiently cope. It was about that time, Cary remembered Kayo saying, he began to blame the war. As Kayo grew more resentful of the war's impact on his father's life, he also grew to hate that his name was connected to war in any way.

Cary reached to his night stand and opened the drawer. He felt around and pulled out a well-worn paperback book. He clutched it to his chest, hugging it like a security blanket. His crossed arms hid the title, *Rules for Radicals*, and the author's name, Saul Alinsky, while he lingered in that position. As Cary lifted the book so he could gaze at the cover, a photograph fell out. It was taken on a hill overlooking a river flowing away from the site. Overhead a bridge traversed the river. Cary flipped the picture over. "Taken at The Pub, Summer 1973" was written in blue ink on the back. Below that it said, "Thanx for helping me see things more clearly and showing me where we are going." It was signed, "Kayo."

Cary flashed on the first time he met Kayo at the University of Columbiana in Oakville, two hours from Columbiana City, in early 1971. Cary was enrolled, not taking a full load of classes, to give himself more time for anti-war activism. Kayo stumbled upon an anti-war rally, met Cary, and ended up crashing with him and several others. Cary immediately saw that he could exploit Kayo's anger and naiveté and manipulate and persuade him to get more seriously involved in the movement. He took advantage of Kayo's youth and inexperience, fueled the young student's anti-war feelings to a new level, and turned his new friend into an activist against the bloody, impossible-to-win war in Vietnam.

Cary laid the photograph on his chest and recalled that he had intended for Kayo to do more of the dirty work, his dirty work. Kayo did not put up much resistance. Cary placed his hand on the photograph and remembered convincing Kayo to set off a smoke bomb in the back of a political science class and how he had instructed Kayo to escape without getting caught. *How did he get away with that?* Cary asked himself.

But as soon as Kayo was hooked, Cary realized he genuinely liked the kid, pulled back a bit on the manipulations, and took on a caring, protective, almost older brother role. For a moment, Cary stopped reminiscing. He wiped mistiness from his eyes.

Looking at the photograph of the river again, Cary observed how unobstructed the view was. *The shrubs and trees have grown so much since then,* he thought. Cary fiddled with the corner of the picture and remembered thinking that from the beginning of their friendship he had had a dominant role, a power position. Two years older than Kayo, Cary was also physically much darker than Kayo in both hair color and complexion, more striking in appearance. *People always said I was so confident and cocky,* he thought as he began to chuckle. *I was always able to get people to do shit.* He paused. *Hey, I talked Kayo into joining our little group of rebels, didn't I?*

Cary inserted the picture in the book, leaned over, replaced it on the nightstand, and fell back on the mattress. He gazed at the ceiling again. Cary started to think about his own family. Like Kayo's father, Cary's had fought in World War II. But Nate Foreman hadn't served on the front lines; he was an army mechanic, always serving his troops and the nation from a safe, relatively speaking, distance. He was never injured in the war. He came home, opened a service station, and married his high school sweetheart. Nate and Louise had Robert first, who eventually became a bus driver, then Cary, and finally Darlene who went to college to get a "Mrs." degree.

Cary's thoughts returned to his anti-war activities. He managed to remain underground, unknown to investigative reporters, the police, and the FBI by avoiding visible leadership roles at demonstrations and civil disobediences. He was always blending in with the masses, dodging cameras and eluding the spotlight. He again wiped mistiness from his eyes.

Cary reached for the book on the nightstand, but stopped. Cary recalled how Kayo's eventual arrest panicked him. It triggered a bout of paranoia. If law enforcement could connect Kayo to the bombing, or any incident, Cary felt, they certainly could connect Kayo to him. Cary expected the inevitable knock on the door or sidewalk ambush during those first days after his friend's arrest. He expected to be arrested.

But he wasn't.

Cary looked at the ceiling. *What was worse?* he reflected, *getting arrested or waiting and waiting and not getting arrested?* News accounts of the bombing, Kayo's arrest and resulting prison sentence never mentioned Cary. *It didn't make sense to me then and it still doesn't,* thought Cary.

Cary flashed on a conversation he had had with Lisa years later. "Didn't you ever feel guilt or remorse for what you did?" she asked over dinner one breezy Honolulu night.

"No. Not really," Cary replied. "The bombings, the disruptions, and the damage had to be done. No. I never regretted any of that."

"But what about Kayo?" Lisa rephrased her question.

"Oh, Kayo." Cary swallowed. He looked down. "Yes. Of course I have regrets regarding him," Cary admitted. "From the moment they read the verdict, *I* felt guilty. He wouldn't have been in that mess if it hadn't been for me." Cary tapped his spoon on the table. "I never turned myself in or tried to share the blame for the bombing," Cary said louder. "I never tried to save Kayo's ass, Lisa."

So Cary laid low, kept quiet, and suffered deep paranoia and guilt.

Several weeks after the trial ended and Kayo was moved to a federal prison, Cary risked it all. He trimmed his hair, dressed in black slacks, a white dress shirt, and a conservative gray tie, and went to visit Kayo. At the prison gate, he showed a fake ID which identified him as Edsel Rosenberg of Stover. Once inside the prison, Cary was again asked to show his ID. This time he added his business card, which informed the reader that Edsel (Ed) Rosenberg was a counselor-at-law. The fake credentials, which had been procured through a supportive printer friend, were accepted without question.

Kayo looked shocked to see Cary through the visitor's window, Cary remembered. "What are you doing here?" Kayo whispered through a combination of clenched teeth and forced smile. "And looking like that. You need to go. Now. Go. Get away. We don't know each other. You have no connection to me." He paused. His tone changed to a more reassuring one. "Hey, I'm OK, man," he said a bit louder. "I'll be OK. I'll see you whenever. But I will see you again. Now go." He took a breath. His natural smile appeared. "It's good to see you. Now get the hell out of here." Then Kayo stood, turned and walked away without looking back.

Cary, shifting his position in his bed, sighed.

The memory of his leaving town two days later, paranoia and guilt packed between his faded, tattered, jeans, lay next to him in the sagging double bed. He went first to Honolulu for a week, and then to Poipu Beach, Kauai, where he connected with a high school classmate, Danny Cavendish, who was working at a hotel as a shuttle and charter bus driver. Manipulative, persuasive Cary used Danny to get a job as a dish washer in the hotel's restaurant. Cary felt safe there. For the mid-1970s, Poipu Beach was about as far off the grid as one could get from Columbiana.

If Cary had been an under-the-radar activist before he fled to Hawaii, he was even more unnoticeable in Kauai. He worked at the restaurant, went home to his tiny apartment, and saved his money. He purposely made no friends, socialized privately with Danny only, and stayed as far away from activism, crime, and the police as he could.

After a year of saving money, Cary returned to Honolulu where, while working at a Waikiki convenience store, he met Lisa Carney. They became inseparable and were married a year later. Shortly after that, he enrolled in the University of Hawaii. To distance himself from his radical past, Cary opted to start college all over, forfeiting the few credits he'd earned at the University of Columbiana, leaving the Foreman transcripts buried in a mainland file cabinet. He enrolled as Cary Carney, taking Lisa's name which he hoped would throw off investigators searching for Cary Foreman. If he were asked why he took Lisa's name, he would lie and say, "It's a feminist statement." He eventually earned his

Bachelor of Arts in History and then began work on attaining a teaching degree, completing the leap from counterculture to establishment.

Cary plumped his pillow, reached for his copy of *Rules for Radicals*, pulled the photograph from it, and stared at the ceiling for a moment. He looked down at the picture and flipped it over. He studied Kayo's inscription. *I did help him understand things,* he thought. *Like Lisa did for me.* Then a vision of Lisa appeared. *Oh, I wish you'd met Kayo, babe.*

Cary turned the photograph over and looked at the river. *That river is life,* he philosophized. *It is flowing toward something, moving forward.* Cary recalled how, just days after he received his teaching certificate, Lisa gave birth to Nick. *We had an ideal life,* he thought. *First, just you and me, babe. Then we had Nick and it became even more perfect,* Cary reminisced. And then, rather quickly, Lisa died of ovarian cancer. Tears rolled past his crow's feet and onto his pillow. He wiped his eyes with the pastel yellow sheet. Yellow had been Lisa's favorite color.

The pain of Lisa's death lingered. Cary remembered he was on the staff of a new community college at the time of Lisa's death. Nick was fifteen when his mother died. He did not handle it well. *I handled it worse,* Cary gazed upward, *and that didn't help Nick at all.* Three years later, when Nick graduated from high school, Cary announced he had never been able to overcome the pain of losing Lisa. To avoid living where all their memories together were, he took a new position at a community college in Columbiana City. "I'm going home," he told Nick with tepid excitement. It was 1999.

Nick remained in Honolulu because it was, as he told his dad, "the only home I've ever known and it's perfect." The distance between Honolulu and Columbiana City would have been enough to challenge Cary and Nick's relationship were it only measured in miles, but time, too, eventually widened the gulf between them. Communication became rare and belabored as the days, months, and years passed. And, unknown to Cary, there was yet another component to the painful estrangement. In an awkward phone call, Nick finally told his father he had felt abandoned when Cary left Hawaii. This, he said, had triggered his anger, resentment, and iciness. "I'm not over it yet, Dad," Nick said.

Aw, Nick, come on, Cary pleaded, as he rose and sat on the edge of the bed. He took *Rules for Radicals* from the nightstand and perused its red and white cover. *It's unbelievable how much the world has changed since I stole this book,* he thought as he replaced the book in the nightstand drawer. Cary stood and walked toward the kitchen. As he passed the bedroom that had become his office, Cary noticed his computer atop an old wooden desk. *I still can't get over how much technology has changed. And it keeps changing.* He walked to the desk and touched the computer's screen.

Cary thought about how he had long resisted many technological advances, like laptops and cell phones. Invasive, he rationalized. Certainly, he used computers at work. In his personal life, however, he avoided them. He told people who tried to push him into New Millennium technologically, he "just didn't need all that crap" or that he "just couldn't understand it all." But that was not the reason.

Cary simply did not trust new technology. He was certain everything he did, or anyone did, on a computer or cell phone was tracked by some Big Brother organization. He acknowledged some would say he was just being paranoid, a holdover from his radical days. But he knew better; he understood his fear of loss of privacy and anonymity was based on his years of hiding, avoiding leaving evidence, keeping secrets, and flying under the radar. *If you can't find me,* he thought, *you can't know what I'm doing.*

While he did use his home desktop for its writing and spreadsheet programs, Cary rarely utilized the computer for email, research, or as a news source. He seldom used the internet. *Too traceable,* he thought. *Too revealing.* He, therefore, continued to rely on traditional newspapers, magazines, and television broadcasts as his primary news sources as he had for decades. Cable providers tracked subscribers viewing habits, he theorized. What could they glean about a viewer who watches mainstream news programs? That could hardly be considered suspicious or subversive.

SATURDAY, FEBRUARY 19, 2011

Cary sat in his recliner thumbing through the *Rolling Stone* that had been on the end table next to it for years. He was searching for the article about "The Protest

Songs of the '60s and '70s." When he found it, a large photograph of a demonstration from the era greeted him. He began to reflect on what Columbiana City and Oakville had been like then and what they were like when he returned in 1999.

It had been twenty-five years since Cary had been in Columbiana City or Oakville. Nothing was the same. People weren't the same. Places weren't the same. Politics wasn't the same. Issues, conditions, and situations had changed. He easily remained distant and uninvolved, keeping his low-profile life. He was, after all, a history professor; he preferred living in the past, not the present.

Until February 2, 2011.

That was the day war was declared. Oh, it was true Al Kirk had used the word "war" first on February 3. But, one could say, the daring legislative action passing gay marriage the day before was provocative and warlike. Opponents of the controversial measure thought so. They also thought the action was part a larger "gay agenda," an agenda they believed would destroy the United States. But who or what started this war is not all that important; it, Cary believed, had always been inevitable. So, February 3 was the day Cary Foremen decided to take a stand, to return to his life of political activism. That was the day he decided America needed to see politics, process, and the establishment challenged 1970s-style again.

When he unexpectedly ran into Kayo Alexander two days later, he knew it was destiny that brought them together. He knew that he and Kayo would team up again. So, as Cary finally crawled out of bed that Sunday morning, and prepared himself to meet Kayo at the place he simply described as "you know where," he was certain his old friend, his compatriot from another time, his brother for life would come.

SUNDAY, FEBRUARY 20, 2011

When Kayo burst through the hillside's green overgrowth, his face displayed surprise and disbelief. "My god this place has changed. The trees are huge. The bushes block everything. I couldn't even find the trailhead." He looked at Cary. "OK. I'm here. But why? Holy shit! There's no view." He looked at Cary again. "OK. Why am I here? Beer cans and bottles. And condom wrappers! They're all over the place. Shit, what a mess." Kayo shook his head. "Not in our day. Maybe a roach or two but that was about it. We kept this place clean. No evidence we'd been here. OK. So why am I here?" he asked for the third time. He looked up at the broad, aging, bridge overhead and its underside. "The bridge is the same, though. The sounds are still the same."

The constant noise of a main arterial – roaring engines, thumping tires, and rattling semis – drowned out any conversation under the bridge. No spies, no witnesses could overhear what was being said, what was being planned. That detail had been intentional in the '70s; it was intentional today. Even the name of this place was cryptic, coded, and misleading. It was called "The Pub," short for Place Under (the) Bridge. "I'll meet you at The Pub" did not mean beer was involved.

"You're here, Kayo," Cary began, "because we have a mission. Something has been going on for a while and now we have to stop it. It is something I think you can relate to. You told me you and Dan were not part of the gay community. You kept to yourselves. Right?"

"Yeah," Kayo responded suspiciously.

"And from what you told me, you loved Dan and he loved you. Right?"

"Yeah."

"Did you ever talk about getting married?"

Kayo snorted a laugh. "Hell, no."

"And why was that? Was it because it wasn't allowed? Because America didn't allow it?"

"Yeah. But what are you getting at, man?"

"Did you ever wish you could have gotten married?"

"No! Gay people didn't get married. It wasn't even considered. It wasn't discussed."

"Did you ever wish you could have gotten married?" Cary repeated.

"No. Not really," Kayo insisted. He paused. A look of recollection came over his face. "Well, actually, yeah, we did talk about it at tax time and when we tried to buy a house. Oh, and when he was in the hospital."

Cary sighed deeply and smiled. "And that is why we are here."

"What?"

"It is time, my friend, for gays and lesbians to be able to get married. They've been pushed around, disrespected, lied about, and denied their rights for way too long. They've made gains, but they've been far too nice, polite, and patient in their fight for equality. The bigots are still out there. It is time for you and me to show gay rights activists how it is done and silence the hate-filled opposition once and for all."

"And you want me to be a part of this?" Kayo asked. "I don't think I can. I'm too old. You're too old."

"But we're experienced, Kayo. And smart. Look at all the shit we did, pulled off. We almost got away with 100 percent, man. We were a great team. We could be one again."

"No. It's someone else's turn. Besides, I don't have a compelling personal reason to get involved."

"Of course you do."

"I do? What? I'm not going to be getting married. Not at my age. Not as a gay man who is not part of the community. Not as an old gay man without any romantic prospects." Kayo looked down.

"Your reason is in one word, *Dan*. Think about all the times you got fucked over doing taxes. Think about all the times you had to lie on forms for, I don't know, credit cards, insurance. What about when he died, Kayo? How did the system treat you then?"

Kayo looked up. A nerve had been struck. He stared past Cary, at the overgrown shrubs blocking the view of the river, weighing his options. He stopped and gazed upward again at the bridge's underside, beyond it, skyward. He turned to Cary. "If I were to say yes," he tentatively asked, "what would happen next?"

Suddenly, as if scripted, a great rustling shook the trees and shrubs where the trail exited the woods onto the open meeting area. Cary and Kayo turned quickly to face the commotion. A gray-haired woman appeared, a bit flustered.

"Oh, thank god you're still here. Sorry I'm late. The bus ran late." Her eyes locked on Kayo. "Oh, I don't believe it! Kayo. Look at you!"

Before Kayo could gather his wits, the woman was hugging him like a long lost friend, which he was. "Let me look at you," Kayo said, as he pulled himself from the embrace. "Jules, you haven't changed." He cackled his signature laugh. "Oh my god, do you know how many times I've thought of you over the years?"

"Of course I've changed. I'm old and gray and I'm at least thirty-five pounds heavier. And I'll bet you've thought of me half as often as I've thought of you."

She pulled Kayo into a second, even firmer embrace. As they separated, she shrieked, "Kayo, you still have your ponytail!" She pulled it playfully.

Julietta Zelenkas, Jules, had met Cary in the late 1960s. They shared a common hatred for the war in Vietnam and became immediate friends. But it wasn't until the early '70s that they transitioned from bystanders to anti-war activists. *Activists* was too lenient a word; *radicals* was more appropriate.

Jules was born July 5, 1948, a day late, she would say, to be a Yankee Doodle Dandy. Because she was a few years older than the others in Cary's crowd, she became a mother figure and it seemed appropriate. Physically, she was the prototype earth-mother. Zaftig, rumpled, and makeup free, Jules wore her mousy brown hair in a long braid, often plopped messily on her head. She was known for her abundance of peasant blouses, and denim dresses, and for her skill in the kitchen. She worked as a costumer and makeup artist for Columbiana's primary theater group.

"Jules, I've been trying to find you for years. I Googled your name a hundred times at least," Kayo said.

"I'm Sternberg now. I dropped Zelenkas thirty years ago. I never married Wayne, but was with him for years and I took his name. We have a grown daughter."

"No way," Kayo said.

"Eden was a tomboy from birth and came out at sixteen. She and her partner Jessica moved to Chicago where Eden is an auto mechanic. Jessica is a firefighter."

"Really." Kayo tilted his head. "Hey, why are you here anyway?" A beat passed. "Oh, I get it. You two have been plotting behind my back, haven't you? And if you, Cary, couldn't convince me to get on board, you brought in the big guns to talk me into it 'cuz you know I can't say no to Jules. I never could. She's my mama and I love her."

"Exactly, man. Now you can't say no."

"OK. So like I asked before we were so rudely interrupted" — Kayo looked at Jules and smiled — "what's next?"

"Finally!" Cary exploded. He lunged forward and hugged Kayo tighter than he had at Starbuck's, tighter than he had hugged anyone in years. "You have no idea how much I worried about you, missed you, man. Neither of us really understands how much we've missed doing this kind of shit, the excitement of creating chaos and raising hell."

"So what's next?" Kayo repeated, this time with urgency.

"Are you aware of what's going on with gay marriage in this state? You are, aren't you?"

"Well, of course. The legislature passed a bill or something. The governor signed it. It's a done deal."

"And we're gonna make sure it stays that way, a done deal." Cary looked at Kayo quizzically. "You don't know, you don't realize that the people opposed to gay marriage, and gay rights in general for that matter, intend to put this matter on the ballot? They want the public to vote on gay marriage, to overturn the legislature and governor. One of their spokesmen said signing the gay marriage bill would trigger a culture war. He used the word 'war.' That is a direct threat. They're kicking off their campaign tomorrow. You know it'll be filled with lies and hate."

"No. I didn't know all of that, not all the details. But I do know there are forces against gay people. I'm not stupid. I just thought this law was a done deal."

"Did you know about the bombing at Snakes on Valentine's Day? Two people died and one is hanging onto life by a thread."

"Yes. Of course I know about that," Kayo answered.

"Man, do you think it was a coincidence that happened on the day Governor Oleson signed the marriage bill? Hell, no. I don't know for sure if the group filing the initiative tomorrow in Stover was involved in that bombing, but the two things are connected. They have to be stopped. All of them."

"OK," Kayo said. But passion and commitment were absent from his voice. "So what's the plan, Mr. Foreman?"

TUESDAY, FEBRUARY 22, 2011

Columbiana's Number One News Source--KEHT Channel 8--February 22, 2011--Initiative to Stop Gay Marriages Filed streamed across the television screen as *The News @ 5* intro and shrill musical theme ended and anchor Lacey Powers appeared.

"Anti-gay marriage forces filed an initiative today that would temporarily block gay marriages and put the entire issue on November's ballot," Lacey reported after greeting the program's viewers. "They have until midnight, June 15 to collect 163,000 signatures. We go now to Kimberly Teller in Stover who has talked with leaders on both sides of this contentious issue. Good evening, Kimberly. What can you tell us about the initiative and the events of the day?"

"Good evening, Lacey. Yes, before the initiative was filed, longtime anti-gay minister Al Kirk held a press conference announcing the formation of the group heading the initiative drive."

Footage from that morning appeared on the screen. A nearly unrecognizable Al Kirk dressed as Uncle Sam stood at a bank of microphones in front of the building housing the Secretary of State's office. "I am here on George Washington's birthday," Kirk proclaimed, "to announce the formation of SAM, Save America's Marriages, to end this talk of homosexual marriage once and for all." A crowd of supporters facing him cheered and held up signs reading "One Man, One Woman." Wedding bands formed the capital O's. "We are tired of having our marriages mocked, our true American values ridiculed, and being forced to accept gays and their agenda as if they and it are normal. We are filing an initiative that will stop these non-marriages. We are confident we will collect the signatures necessary, trigger an overwhelming win at the ballot box for real marriages everywhere, and end this sham. I am proud to announce that Sandi Iglesias, president of the League of American Women, LAW,"…and the camera pulled back to include a woman cradling a gaudy ceramic American Eagle in her arms…"will serve as my co-chairman."

Just as the smiling Sandi Iglesias stepped to the microphone to speak to the crowd of cheering supporters, a powerful explosion erupted in back of the audience. Startled, Sandi dropped the eagle, shattering it. KEHT's camera swung around to capture the source of the noise, but recorded, instead, members of the crowd turning toward the explosion, while others immediately scattered, screaming or protecting their heads with their hands from expected shards of debris.

In the distance, all that appeared near the blast site was a large stream of shocking pink smoke. A moment later, a second blast roared from the far end of the stoic stone building. The camera turned to show lavender smoke wafting heavenward from that explosion. Disorganized security guards rushed toward both sites, unsure what to look for or what to do. Unnoticed, Al Kirk and an emotionally shattered Sandi Iglesias hurried to the Secretary of State's office.

"As you can see, Lacey," Kimberly said as her image returned to the screen, "there was a bit of a disruption. No one was injured."

"Do we know who or what was responsible for the smoke bombs?"

"The police are investigating. We do know they were caused by simple homemade incendiary devices," the reporter answered.

"Did the speakers return? Were they able to finish their announcement?"

"No," Kimberly said. "A witness told me he saw them huddled in a corner praying."

"Have pro-gay marriage forces responded to today's events, Kimberly?"

"Yes, Lacey. They are represented here today. I spoke earlier with gay rights activist Davis Wells who told me a group is being formed to combat the initiative. No on Discrimination or NOD will hold a press conference Monday, he said."

As she finished that statement, a video clip of Kimberly holding a microphone in front of a business-like, middle-aged man appeared.

"We are not afraid of this initiative or these people, Kimberly," Wells said. "We actually welcome the opportunity to tell our stories, to share our humanity to Columbiana voters statewide. We will conduct ourselves with dignity and calm. We believe Columbiana citizens are too savvy, too wise, and too fair to support this initiative. When they hear our message, they will agree with the legislature and governor and will allow all tax-paying citizens equal marriage rights. There is no room in the State of Columbiana for discrimination." Wells spoke, calmly and professionally. He sounded well-rehearsed.

Kimberly reappeared live on the screen. "That is all from Stover. Kimberly Teller, KEHT News."

"Thank you, Kimberly. In a related story, a previously unseen security camera video from a service station has been turned in that may show the getaway car racing from the Snakes bombing on Valentine's Day. Mike Ross, who owns independent service station PetroMall discovered the images on a security camera. 'Maybe investigators will see something on the film that will help solve the bombing,' he added."

WEDNESDAY, FEBRUARY 23, 2011

"Hi, Cary. It's Kayo. Who set off those smoke bombs in Stover yesterday?"

"I was just gonna ask you the same thing."

"I wonder who did."

"Well," Cary theorized, "there could be others out there who are just as pissed off as we are."

"But if it were gay rights activists, gay marriage activists, Cary, their tactics are just like they've always been. Too nice. Too timid. So they set off pink and lavender smoke bombs. So what. That ain't gonna stop anybody. It ain't gonna scare anybody. At best, maybe two garbage cans were damaged." Kayo snorted a syllable of laughter. "You know, man, they really do need us to shake things up a bit."

Cary, deep in thought, did not hear Kayo's last comment. "Of course, those smoke bombs could have been set off by Al Kirk and his people. What are they called? SAM?" he suggested. "They could have done it to make the public think we did it, that *we* are the threat to society, the ones taking their freedom of speech and freedom of religion away. They could have done it just to turn people against us from the get-go." Cary's tone changed. "But listen, man, we shouldn't be having this conversation on the phone. We have to have it privately. You know where. Tomorrow at ten. I want to introduce you to some people, some awesome people."

"You're right, man," Kayo paused. "'Awesome people'? That piques my curiosity. See you then."

THURSDAY, FEBRUARY 24, 2011

Kayo was at The Pub by himself waiting to meet Cary's "awesome people." When hushed voices from the trail seeped through the overgrowth and rustling branches, Kayo faced the direction of the noise with anticipation. Cary was the first to step through the shrubs, followed by three younger people, two men and a woman.

"Guys," Cary announced, "this is the famous, or infamous, Kayo Alexander." He walked toward Kayo, slung his arm over Kayo's shoulder, and faced the trio. "That is Adam Shapiro on the end. He works in the city's records office. And he's my neighbor. He'll be a great asset finding information on people. That's his partner, Stevon Franklin," he said, motioning to a tall African American, "He works at Home Depot in electrical supplies. He knows wiring and explosives. Can you imagine what a help he'll be? And this incredible woman is Bren Dailey, a techie and internet detective. Something we didn't need in the '70s but, shit, is so vital today."

Adam, Stevon, and Bren converged on Kayo, shaking his hand, patting him on the back, and expressing how happy and excited they were to meet him. All three appeared to be in their mid-twenties.

Cary got right to business, explaining motives, roles, and goals. "You three haven't met Jules. But she is crucial to our team," he began. "Her makeup and wig styling skills and access to costumes are so, so important. She isn't here, though, because she flew to Chicago to convince her daughter Eden and her partner Jess to join us," Cary said. "Having a mechanic and firefighter on the team would be great."

"So," Bren asked, "what is our plan, Cary? You've told us in a general sense what our purpose is, what our tactics will be, but you haven't really shared details or specifics."

"As you know, Al Kirk said, 'We will fight this war.' He used the word 'war' first. So we aren't starting the war," Cary replied. "We're just defending ourselves. So here's my battle plan."

THURSDAY, MARCH 3, 2011

Shop-Wright, the leading chain of supermarkets in Columbiana, is owned by the wealthy, politically conservative Wright Family. Emboldened by family scion Zebulon Wright's immediate $100,000 contribution to Save America's

Marriages, it was no surprise that SAM leaders urged initiative signature gatherers to utilize Shop-Wright parking lots throughout the state whenever possible. They had begun collecting signatures on March 1.

Two days later, as two signature gatherers asked shoppers to sign their petition, a middle-aged woman named Abby watched them from her generic, aging compact car parked across the suburban store's sprawling lot. She observed an elderly man and a young woman with a preschooler in tow approach shoppers. Many shoppers brushed past the duo. Some stopped and listened politely to what the signature gatherers had to say, but declined to sign the initiative. Numerous shoppers signed the petition on the spot, many without even listening to the presentation the two petitioners were prepared to give.

Abby studied the scene. Two card tables had been pushed together. On the tables lay several clipboards with, she assumed, initiatives on them. A box sat under the table on the right, apparently serving as the depository for completed forms. The man and woman, with her young son following closely, carried other clipboards. They also had fliers which they handed to interested passersby.

Abby left the shelter of her car and headed to the store's entrance. As she passed the elderly man, Abby heard his spiel presented to a woman and noticed the man had an American flag pin and a military decoration on his jacket lapel. *Nice touch*, she thought, as the female signature gatherer approached, smiling.

"Excuse me, ma'am," the political volunteer said. "Would you like to sign our initiative to stop gay marriage?"

Abby reacted with a faux-naïve curiosity. "And how would it do that?"

"If we get enough signatures, the issue will go on November's ballot. Then we can stop gay marriage and save America's marriages." The SAM woman went on. "Aren't you getting tired of the gay rights radicals cramming their agenda down everyone's throat? It is destructive for families. She looked down at the boy and patted his head. On cue, the boy smiled like an angel at the potential initiative signer. The woman held out a clipboard and pen.

Abby looked directly into the SAM woman's eyes and quietly asked, "Who the fuck do you think you are?" Then she raised her voice. "That's all bullshit!"

Startled by the choice of words and tone, the SAM mom grabbed her little boy's hand and pulled him away. But Abby, now on the offense, would not be silenced. She rushed after the mother and son, stepped in front of them, and crouched down to the boy's eye level.

"Your mother is a fucking liar. Don't ever believe anything she says," she ordered. "Ever. She lies." The mother pulled her son behind her while Abby ranted on. "If your mom ever told you she loves you, it was a lie. She doesn't love you."

With that final blast, Abby rose and raced to her car. The male signature gatherer ran to his shocked political partner who was hugging her now sobbing son. The smattering of shoppers in the parking lot looked on with confusion and disbelief. Only one had the wherewithal to pull out his cell phone and photograph the fleeing car as it sped out of the lot.

Later that day, as the intro and theme of KEHT's *The News @ 5* ended and anchor Mac Hines greeted viewers, a bold graphic announcing "Breaking News" filled the TV screen. "This is an exclusive! We lead off tonight's news with a confrontation this morning in a supermarket parking lot. Our Kimberly Teller is there. Good evening, Kimberly."

"Good evening, Mac," the reporter responded as *Gay Marriage Confrontation at Supermarket. Attack Shocks Signature Gatherer* repeatedly ran across the base of the screen. "Yes, a loud confrontation did occur this morning here at the Shop-Wright in Linnton. It appears to have been between a volunteer collecting signatures to have the gay marriage act halted and an angry bystander. The volunteer, Carla Valenti, was quite shaken by the incident."

Video of a clearly emotional woman appeared on screen. "All of a sudden this woman was screaming at me," she said with a shaky voice, "and using language I can't repeat. And she was saying all this in front of my four-year-old son. Then she crossed the line."

"What did she do?" Kimberly, off-camera, asked.

"It was horrible. She started yelling at James, telling him I was a liar and that I didn't love him." Then Carla Valenti broke down sobbing. The camera cut from the video to Kimberly live.

"An alert bystander watched the screaming woman race to her car and tear out of the lot," Kimberly said. "He managed to take a picture of the car's license plate with his cell phone. He then contacted KEHT and we were able to track down the woman."

Another video filled the screen. Kimberly was standing at the front door of a small, wooden house with blistered, beige paint. Overgrown bushes crowded her. The door opened slightly and a blurred figure peeked around it.

"Ms. Hoffman? Are you Abigail Hoffman?" the reporter asked.

"Abby. Yes."

"We understand you were involved in a verbal confrontation at Shop-Wright earlier today. Can you tell us what happened?"

Abby opened the door wider but remained inside, her hand on the knob. "They were collecting signatures to stop gay men and lesbians from marrying and they were telling lies, nothing but lies. They've been telling those homophobic lies for years, decades. I am sick of it. They cannot get away with spreading their hate any more. No more of their lies. No more of their discrimination. No more of their slandering a whole group of people and the individuals who make up that group."

A dog barked in the distance. A gust of wind caused the overgrown bushes next to the porch to sway. A car horn honked.

"Do you think you went perhaps a little too far, drawing James Valenti into this political battle?"

"Who?"

"The little boy. The volunteer's little boy," Kimberly clarified.

"Hell, no," Abby snapped. "She brought him to — what did you just call this? — 'this political battle.' Besides, how many young boys and girls just beginning to understand their homosexuality have been told by people like that woman that they were sinners and that God hated them. How many? And for how many decades? Oh, no. I didn't go any further than they have."

With that, angry Abby Hoffman slammed the door. "I'm done with this bullshit," she yelled from inside the house. KEHT did not censor her last word.

Kimberly appeared live again. "I've asked police if any crime was committed here today. A spokesperson says because no one was assaulted and no property damaged, probably not. Back to you in the studio, Mac."

"Well, the battle regarding gay marriage is certainly heating up," the anchorman said. "And in other news today, a city councilman has an unusual plan to revive downtown."

FRIDAY, MARCH 4, 2011

"Did any of you see the news last night? The woman who confronted the SAM signature gatherer?" Cary asked. Kayo, Cary, Jules, Bren, and Stevon, who sat in a circle on the patch of littered lawn under the bridge, nodded. "Her name is Abby Hoffman. But who is she? We gotta get her on board! We need her anger, her passion."

"Adam's working on it," Stevon announced. "We have a connection at KEHT that may be able to tell us how to contact Abby. Even though car license plates are a state thing, Adam has access the DMV at work for cross-referencing. He's at his office now, working on it."

"You have a connection at KEHT?" Kayo and Cary blurted in unison.

"To be kept under cover. Adam and I are working it."

As that conversation was being held at The Pub, Adam picked up his office phone and dialed. "Hi," he said quietly. "Call me later, after I get home."

SATURDAY, MARCH 5, 2011

"Don't make me go to work today," Stevon pleaded as he lay naked in bed cuddled next to Adam. He was nestled in Adam's arm, his head resting on Adam's shoulder. Adam's hand lay across Stevon's flat, caramel-colored stomach, his index finger drawing tiny patterns on it. "Home Depot can survive without me. I just want to stay here, right here, all day."

"You have to be there by ten," Adam said.

"So that means there's time to do it again. Only it's my turn this time."

"I know. I love it when it is your turn," Adam replied.

With permission given, Stevon scrambled between Adam's legs, sat up on his knees, and looked down at his partner of five years. "You are so fucking hot, babe. God, I love you," he said. As he leaned over and kissed Adam hard, yet tenderly, the back of Adam's head pushed his pillow and the mattress down far enough to squash the dust bunnies under their bed.

Twenty-five minutes later, Adam was in the kitchen brewing the Saturday morning coffee and Stevon was showering when the morning quiet was rattled by Lady Gaga's "Poker Face," Adam's cell phone ringtone. It was just after nine.

"Hello," Adam answered.

"Hi. Sorry I didn't call back last night. Couldn't. I got home too late. Who knew when I took on this assignment at work, it would develop so quickly? So what did you call about? Are you and Stevon OK?"

"Yes, we're OK. We're always OK." A satisfied smile came over Adam's face as he looked toward the bedroom. "It's about what happened Thursday at Shop-Wright. That signature collector sure came off as the victim. And the other woman, Abigail Hoffman, seemed just a wee bit angry. And crazy. Did you have to do such a good job being fair and balanced?"

"Well, never let it be said that Kimberly Teller is a biased reporter." There was a pause. "Oh, I know. You want the dish on her."

"Of course I do. Who is she? How do we get in touch with her?" Adam asked urgently.

"I'll bring the contact information over later this morning. But remember, this is confidential. I could get royally screwed for being involved in this."

"I know. We all appreciate any help you can give us. Thanks, Mom."

TUESDAY, MARCH 8, 2011

Third Death from Snakes Bombing read the crawl as KEHT's *Morning News* returned from a commercial break. Lacey Powers, with her usual abundance of makeup and overly teased and sprayed hair, looked seriously at the camera.

"A third victim of the Valentine's Day bombing at Snakes has died," Lacey stated somberly. "Tom Sandberg passed away late last night at County General where he'd been in a coma since the bombing. Sandberg was a popular drag queen and avant-garde performance artist known as Tamara Today. Friends announced a memorial is planned for his birthday April 9. No arrests have been made in the bombing."

That's my birthday, too, Cary thought as he bit into a warm, buttered onion bagel.

The anchor turned and looked off-camera as the shot pulled back to show traffic reporter Amber Nguyen in front of a red and green traffic map. "Good morning, Amber," Lacey chirped. "What's happening on the roads this Tuesday morning? Your map looks all Christmassy."

"Well, if it does, Lacey, I suppose the red areas represent all the children getting coal this year. And the green? Maybe the money the good kids will get." Amber and Lacey laughed as if Tom Sandberg's death and traffic accidents were funny and appropriate for a comedy routine.

THURSDAY, MARCH 10, 2011

Breaking News! repeatedly raced across the television screen as KEHT's *NoonNews8* began. *Arrests Made in Snakes Bombing.*

"Good afternoon," Mac Hines said more quickly than normal. "We have breaking news. Two suspects in the Valentine's Day bombing of Snakes, a local gay dance club, were arrested just minutes ago. They are being transported to the county jail as we speak. Kimberly Teller is there. Good afternoon, Kimberly. What do we know about the suspects?"

"Good afternoon, Mac. All we have been told is that the suspects are foreigners and that a third suspect is still at large."

"Do we know what nationality?"

"We were not told that."

"Do we know if these alleged foreigners are longtime residents or recent arrivals?"

"We haven't been told that. The arrests were just made and details are still quite sketchy." Kimberly paused. "Hopefully, we will have more information for *The News @ 5.*"

Kimberly did have more details for the late afternoon newscast. Cary watched it from the back of the MetComm Student Lounge. A smattering of students sat throughout the room. Some were watching the broadcast. Others studied. But most were lost in the private worlds of their cell phones, handheld electronic devices, and headphones or earbuds. Cary stood next to Derek Stone, a much younger history professor whose office was next to Cary's. Both men stared at the television more intently than any of the students in the room. Overfilled briefcases dangled from each of their right arms.

"The two arrested suspects are Columbiana City residents Vladimir Turgenov and Kirill Plotkin. A third suspect, Andrei Smirnov, is still at large and may have left the country," Kimberly Teller began her updated report. "Turgenov and Plotkin are twenty-seven and twenty-five respectively and are naturalized U.S. citizens, having emigrated from Russia with their families in the mid-1990s. Smirnov is a younger cousin of Turgenov and was visiting the U.S. when the bombing occurred. Investigators believe Turgenov and Smirnov set the bomb, while Plotkin drove the getaway car. The car, it was revealed, was located after a service station security camera captured the license plate number. It is registered to Plotkin and it was found abandoned in a Columbiana International Airport parking lot. It is believed Smirnov returned to Russia after the bombing while the other two, since they had not been seen recently, left the area to escape arrest. They apparently returned yesterday, perhaps thinking it was safe; police immediately had them under surveillance."

Professor Stone looked at Cary, nodded, and returned his focus to the television.

"They will appear," Kimberly concluded, "in Superior Court tomorrow and are charged with three counts of first degree murder along with a variety of lesser charges."

"Thank you, Kimberly," Mac said. "We'll be in the courtroom tomorrow when the two men make their first appearance. Meanwhile, in other news, a broken water main flooded an Eastside neighborhood today."

"It was horrible when it happened, the bombing," Stone said as he and Cary began walking to their offices. "Unthinkable. My brother could have been there. It seems to get worse as time goes by and details are uncovered."

"I know. I hope they get that third guy," Cary replied.

FRIDAY, MARCH 11, 2011

As Vladimir Turgenov and Kirill Plotkin pleaded "not guilty" to a litany of serious charges in Columbiana City's courthouse, Andrei Smirnov sent an email to them. "Are you still in Canada?" he wrote in Russian. "When do you think it will be safe for you to go home? Is everything OK?"

Police investigators, coincidently, were in the process of confiscating Turgenov's laptop when the message arrived. Within an hour, lead investigator Lt. Jason Yamamoto had secured the services of a Russian translator, who told the policeman in an off-hand manner that Kirill is Russian for Cyril.

"You mean like in the Cyrillic Alphabet? You mean like St. Cyril, the founder of the Russian Orthodox Church? Yamamoto asked.

"Yes."

The lieutenant also contacted an internet detective, a part-time department employee. "Can you be here in the morning? I realize tomorrow is Saturday, but we've got the laptop and have an email we urgently need to trace."

"Yep. I'll be there," Bren Daily answered.

SATURDAY, MARCH 12, 2011

Adam Shapiro burst through the wet shrubs. A light overnight rain had dampened the bushes' tangled branches and made the trail a bit slippery. A woman, wearing a faded "McGovern '72" T-shirt, followed Adam. She seemed to be about forty and smaller than she had appeared on TV. She stopped abruptly when she exited the overgrowth and stepped into The Pub. Cary was already there, facing them.

"This is Abigail Hoffman, Cary," Adam announced. "She goes by Abby. Abby, that's Cary."

"What you did in that parking lot, Abby, was awesome," Cary said without a greeting. "When you were interviewed on the news, your anger and passion came through loud and clear. So much so, in fact, I thought we need people with that kind of anger and passion to help us."

"Who is 'we' and 'us'?" interrupted Abby. "Adam hasn't told me much about you or this meeting. I'll admit I was curious and agreed to come, but I kind of feel like I've been kidnapped."

"Oh, no. You can leave at any time, Abby. I just wanted to meet you and ask if you'd be interested in fighting SAM and that fucking initiative. That's who 'we' are, a small group opposed to discrimination, hate, and homophobia, a small group for fairness and equality."

"But why am I meeting you here and not at a Starbuck's?"

"Because," Adam interjected, "we are a bit…private."

"Secretive," added Cary. "We work under the radar. We are not the establishment, Abby. We are not Davis Wells and No on Discrimination."

"What does that mean?"

"It means," said Adam, "we take risks. We don't always play it safe. It means we make strong statements, not politically correct ones, just like you did that day at the Shop-Wright."

"Well, is what you do, um, um, legal?"

"An interesting question, Abby," Cary asked. "A better one would be, 'Is it morally right? Or necessary? Or effective?' What we do, Abby, we believe, needs to be done."

Abby looked at Cary and then at Adam. She began to toe the dirt with her left foot. She stepped away from the two men and looked up at the bridge. She looked down and slowly turned toward the men. She took a deep breath. "Guys," she said," I'm flattered that you would be interested in my help. But this sounds risky. Part of me says this is too scary. But part of me is very intrigued by the possibilities. I need time to think about this."

"Fair enough," Cary said. "We just ask you keep this meeting, this conversation under cover, Abby. And we think you will. Why? Because we trust you, Abby."

"Why do you trust me? You don't know me."

"True. But we know enough about you. When we learned your name, Adam Googled you."

"Oh," Abby exhaled as if her lungs had been deflated.

"We know that you were involved in the demonstrations in Spain against the Gulf War in 1991. We've seen the pictures of you throwing rocks and smoke bombs at police. Therefore, Abby, hopefully, after you've thought about the offer awhile, you'll join us. You've got Adam's cell number?"

"Yes."

"Then go, think, and decide. But remember, the battle for gay marriage, the *war* for gay marriage," Cary corrected himself, "needs you. We need you, Abby."

"What were you doing in Spain?" Adam asked.

"Providing health care for AIDS patients."

"We know," Cary said with a sly smile.

Abby's laughed nervously, turned and disappeared into the green vegetation around her.

"Dude," Adam said, as the woman disappeared into the greenery, "you like said her name a million times."

"I know," Cary responded. "It is an old strategy I learned years ago."

"What? Being irritating?"

"No. When you use someone's name, you draw them in," Cary explained. "It's psychological. They already think they're accepted, part of whatever it is that is being discussed. It makes it harder for them to say 'no.'"

SATURDAY, MARCH 12, 2011

"Smirnov's email was sent from Krasnoyarsk, Russia," Bren Dailey said, as she burst into Lt. Yamamoto's office. "I've never heard of it. Have you, Jason?" He shook his head. "Anyway, it's in Siberia and has a population of more than a million people."

"As we suspected," the policeman reacted to the news. "He escaped to Russia. Good work, Bren. Can we pin him down more closely?"

"I'm working on it. I have a call out to a Russian computer programmer I met a while back at a conference. He teaches in England. He might be able to help us find Smirnov."

"Well, keep me posted," Yamamoto said.

Lt. Jason Yamamoto was not the only person Bren Dailey kept posted. Immediately upon leaving his office and concealed in a women's restroom, Bren called Cary's home phone and left a message. She then texted Kayo. *Meet me @ The Pub @ 10.*

TUESDAY, MARCH 15, 2011

Poll Shows Gay Marriage Opposed by Columbianans rolled below Mac Hines' face as Cary's television picture appeared. It was several minutes after KEHT's *The 11 O'Clock News* had begun and Cary had just come home from a long day at school.

"Fifty-five percent of voters polled said they would vote to stop the recently signed gay marriage law and support the anti-gay initiative were it to qualify for the November ballot," Mac read. "Thirty-nine percent said they support the law. Six percent were undecided. The survey was conducted by McGraw-Pitts Research. There is a margin of error of four percent."

Cary sighed. "Yep. It's true," he whispered a moment later. "Beware the Ides of March."

FRIDAY, MARCH 25, 2011

Mystery Murder was the headline in *The Krasnoyarskaya Gazeta*. It accompanied a short, detail-challenged article buried deep in the newspaper. It was as if a human's death was unimportant, as if mystery murders were commonplace in the Siberian city.

Kayo never saw the headline, which he would not have understood anyway. He already had returned to Columbiana City from Russia by the time the murder was reported. But he knew all the missing details.

Internet detective Bren Dailey had pinpointed Andrei Smirnov's computer's IP address with relative ease. A residence in Krasnoyarsk was matched to it quite quickly. But Bren wanted to be certain. The name Andrei Smirnov is a rather common one in Russia, comparable to Andrew Smith in English-speaking countries. When research showed that the mother of the match was a Turgenova by birth, the cousin connection became quite clear. Bren was sure she had found the missing conspirator. Before she shared her discovery and information with Lt. Yamamoto, Bren contacted Carey and Kayo and a meeting was called.

Dark clouds filled the sky. Gusty winds blew, causing them to race across the heavens like a "breaking" KEHT headline scrolls across the bottom of Columbiana television screens. The foreboding weather threatened to envelope Cary and Kayo as they awaited Bren at The Pub. The young technology whiz slipped though the wall of green vegetation protecting the meeting place from public exposure as a slash of blue sky split the ominous clouds and then disappeared again. Bren immediately updated the men of her discoveries regarding Andrei Smirnov.

"OK," Cary responded. "Since that asshole will never be tried in the U.S. or Russia for the Snakes murders, I'm going to suggest something rather extreme. This is, and I can't believe I'm using this word, radical. What I'm going to suggest goes beyond anything we did" — and Cary looked directly into Kayo's eyes — "in the '70s." He paused and inhaled slowly. "We have to commit a revenge murder."

Neither Kayo nor Bren reacted with shock. It was as if each had privately, silently considered this action.

"Someone is going to have to go to Krasno…Krasno…"

"…yarsk," Bren completed the name of the Siberian city.

"Yes. Krasnoyarsk," Cary agreed. "I can't; I've got classes until June." He paused and faced his friend. "Kayo, can you do this?"

Kayo gazed straight ahead in contemplation. He shuffled to the bushes in front of him and distractedly fingered a few budding branches. He then looked up past the underside of the bridge as if seeking a message from above. A moment passed. He turned and faced Cary. "Well, I don't know, man. Murder. Commit murder." He closed his eyes and returned to silent contemplation.

"I guess what I am asking, Kayo," Cary interrupted, "really is a twofold question. First, can you do it timewise? Since I can't. But I'm also asking if you can do it…Murder?"

"Yes, I could do it timewise," Kayo said, as if he were more focused on the second question. He closed his eyes a moment and then opened them. "Murder? Commit murder? Well, it's not like I have never thought about this. When I was locked up, I listened to the other guys when they talked about the murders they'd committed. The killings themselves. The motives. The feelings they had afterward. I thought about this very question, the one you just threw at me: Could I kill someone? Cary, I came to the conclusion I could. I could if I were pissed off enough. Or if I felt threatened enough. Or, and it took me a long time to accept this, if I believed it simply needed to be done. Dan and I talked about this a lot. Ironic, isn't it? As much as we had tried to avoid hurting people in the '70s and had stayed away from activism after we got out, we also thought the activists of the '80s and '90s were too tame. They needed to get more serious, more threatening. Time had caused the ante to be raised.

We, Dan and I, evolved. We changed. We became more extreme. Maybe it was a form of Post-Traumatic Stress Disorder. We did see and experience a lot of shit in prison, after all. Maybe we were impacted more deeply by it all than we realized or understood. Maybe we were angrier than we thought." Kayo hung his head and toed a stone in the dirt. "We grew to accept murder as a legitimate course of action under the right circumstances," he said, looking up at Cary again.

"So?"

"So, yes, I could do it, Cary," Kayo replied with growing energy. "Yes," he repeated with more confidence, "I could do it. I will do it," he said, making it official, committing himself to his first murder because, he felt, it had to be done.

Cary grabbed Kayo and hugged him. Bren beamed in the background. "OK," Cary said, as the two men separated. "We have to work fast and we have to work silently, secretly. This conversation does not go beyond us. This plan does not go beyond us. Understood?"

"Understood," Kayo and Bren said together. Without a verbal cue, the trio clasped each other's hands, a group handshake of sorts.

In less than an hour, a plan was drawn up, details forged. Kayo would fly to Krasnoyarsk. Flights were scheduled. Russian money was secured. A Russian dictionary was purchased. Some simple Russian phrases and basic words were learned. A detailed plan was laid out. Since Kayo would not be able to smuggle a gun onto flights, a large kitchen knife would be bought in Krasnoyarsk. To trap Smirnov, Kayo would email him from Russia, introduce himself as a Canadian friend of cousin Vlad, explain he is a student of Russian history on his way to Odessa, and he has a small package from Vlad for him. They had to meet immediately, Kayo would explain, because his layover was short and his flight to the Crimea was early the next afternoon. This concocted urgency, it was hoped, would give Smirnov no time to question or investigate the story.

There was one variable the plan could not control: Smirnov did not live alone. Research uncovered that he shared the address with his parents. His parents, the investigation showed, worked for the same business. What that business was, however, remained a mystery. Its name and purpose were difficult to determine; they appeared to be coded and a bit mysterious, perhaps a cover. The plan, then, was for Kayo to spy on the Smirnov home during the early part of the day prior to the meeting to determine when Smirnov's parents departed for work. Kayo would have to meet the Russian bomber as soon as they left the house.

When Kayo finally arrived a few days later at the pinpointed address, he was wearing a white wig, matching thick mustache, and clear-lensed black-framed glasses. Kayo was quite surprised by what he found. He had expected a modest home or apartment building with tiny, crowded rooms matching what he had seen on television accounts of Russian life. Instead, he found himself in an upper class neighborhood. The Smirnov house was spacious and reflected affluence. He set up a vantage point in a coffee shop almost directly across the street. For two hours, he faked surfing the web on his laptop while he nursed two coffees, one for each hour. While Kayo observed the house, two older model American cars passed by. The first one was a 1972 copper-colored Chevrolet Vega in mint condition. Concentrating on watching the house, Kayo only caught the unexpected older American car in his peripheral vision. When he realized what he had seen and turned to look at it more closely, it was gone. Moments later, another '70s era automobile, a denim blue AMC Gremlin, slowly rambled past the house. By the time Kayo reacted, this car, too, was out of sight, perhaps around a corner. He did not dwell on the odd sightings, however, because he was too focused on the Smirnov home. Finally, after an hour and a half of casing the house, he saw a young man, perhaps nineteen or twenty, step out its front door. He was wearing black running tights, a long sleeve blue T-shirt, and top-of-the-line Nikes. He had headphones over his ears which he adjusted briefly before dashing off, away from Kayo, like an experienced runner. Kayo assumed this was Andrei Smirnov. But he had no proof.

Other than that young man, no one else left or entered the Smirnov home while the jogger was away.

Thirty minutes later, the runner reappeared from the direction in which he had sprinted. Kayo had his proof. This young man was, surely, Andrei Smirnov. Kayo hadn't seen the T-shirt's details when Smirnov had first appeared. But now, as it faced him, "University of Columbiana" complete with the college's logo was distinctly visible. So were large areas of sweat stains.

Kayo left the coffee shop and bought a knife.

Later that day, Kayo sent an email requesting a ten o'clock meeting the next morning. Smirnov replied in minutes. "Yes. Time is good even if I go party tonight," he wrote. "Mother and father in Moscow to do work. So I go out tonight for fun. But I will get out of the bed to see you in morning." Kayo was ecstatic over the response, particularly learning the senior Smirnovs were in Moscow. Nevertheless, he returned to the coffee shop at 8:00 a.m. to observe the home once more and to be certain Smirnov was alone. Kayo wore the wig, mustache, and glasses. Again, no one was seen leaving the house.

Kayo knocked on the heavy wooden door at ten o'clock, holding a small box wrapped in brown paper in his other hand. He was somewhat surprised when Smirnov answered, clad only in pajama bottoms, and was neither shaven nor showered. His dirty blond hair screamed "pillow head."

Smirnov smiled, motioned Kayo inside and shut the door. He placed a *circa* mid-1980s Motorola Mobile Brick Phone on a small table near the door. It appeared well-worn, but seemed to be in working condition. In rather good English, Smirnov apologized for his appearance. "I am young," he said with a laugh. "I go drink last night. I have fun. Especially when mama and papa not here. Nothing for me to worry." He then asked if his cousin was OK.

"Yes, of course. He and Kirill are still working in Vancouver," Kayo lied. "But here is the box." Kayo handed the tightly wrapped and securely taped box to Smirnov. The young man looked at it oddly.

"No name on it," he said as he struggled to find a weak point on the tape.

"Well, it's for you. Vlad gave it to me and said, 'Make sure my cousin gets it.'"

Before Smirnov realized he would need scissors, and with his attention focused on the challenging box, Kayo reached into his thick winter coat's deep inside pocket and pulled out the kitchen knife he'd purchased the day before. Suddenly, he jammed the blade into Smirnov's chest, near his heart. Smirnov's natural reaction was to try to block the unexpected motion toward his body. But he was too late and ineffective. As the Russian dropped the box and grunted, Kayo aimed the knife downward, striking his victim in the lower abdomen, near the base of his penis. This caused Smirnov to double over. Without missing a beat, Kayo rammed the blade upward again, this time spearing the

Russian's heart. Smirnov fell face down on the floor, shock and pain covering his face, moans and gurgling sounds escaping his grimacing mouth. Blood immediately spread across the floor. Kayo struck once more, stabbing the dying man through his bloodied pajama bottoms deep in his rectum. The sounds of violent death ended.

Kayo pushed the still body with his right foot to ascertain it was dead. It did not move. He leaned closer to see if Smirnov was breathing. He was not. Kayo took a quick breath, picked up the impenetrable box, sheathed the bloodied knife in a double-thick plastic Shop-Wright bag, pulled the sleeve of his coat's right arm over his hand to work the door knob without leaving fingerprints, and left.

Once at the corner, Kayo turned and began running until he came to a small park. A lone, elderly woman played ball with a small child at the far end of the park. He turned his back to her, pulled off the white wig, and peeled the mustache from his lip. He was tempted for a moment to keep the nerdy glasses on, but he didn't. Kayo looked around. He saw a banged-up garbage can near the street and dropped the evidence into it. He quickly exited the park, hailed a cab, and returned to the unassuming, cheap hotel at which he had spent the past two nights. Within minutes, he had retrieved his carry-on bag, left the room key on the front counter, jumped into the waiting cab, and headed to Yemelyanova International Airport.

Kayo had timed his escape perfectly. His plane to Moscow lifted off at 1:00 p.m. He took a deep breath as it did, but did not feel totally safe yet. His three-hour Moscow layover was tense and slow. When his Amsterdam-bound flight rose up from the runway, he took two deep breaths. This time he felt relief and safety. He drank vodka to celebrate. Kayo was on the ground in Amsterdam for more than four hours before heading to New York City and then Columbiana City. He had been gone nearly six days. And a lifetime.

SATURDAY, MARCH 26, 2011

"It's done," Kayo told Cary and Bren as they stood at The Pub. It was raining lightly. The bridge overhead served as an umbrella. "I don't think they discovered the body until after I was long gone. His parents were out of town. I did my best to hide evidence, but I'm sure they'll be able to trace my email. There probably is video of me somewhere, with or without the disguise. It is Russia, after all. But I doubt our government would extradite me if requested by the Kremlin."

"Did he put up a fight?" Cary asked.

"I don't want to go into details. I don't even want to talk about it…the actual…event. Maybe never."

"OK."

"Got it," echoed Bren.

"So, what's been happening here while I was traveling?" Kayo asked. He formed quotation marks with his fingers as he said "traveling."

"Surprisingly little," Cary answered. "I feel like it is the calm before the storm."

"Then, may I leave?" Kayo asked. "I'm really tired. I haven't slept well since…" his voice trailed off.

"Of course. Go," Cary answered.

Kayo turned and stepped onto the path leading through the overgrowth and away from The Pub.

Bren waited until Kayo was out of earshot before speaking. "I think that was really hard on him, Cary. Harder than he expected."

"Yeah. But it was something that had to be done. Killing sometimes has to be done, Bren. To win or for self-preservation. Do you think Yankee and Confederate soldiers enjoyed killing one another in the Civil War?" Cary asked rhetorically. "I'm sure they didn't. But they had to do it. Do you think our troops in Vietnam wanted to kill those poor people, those farmers, those innocent civilians? Hell, no. But they either believed they had to do it for the U.S., for the world, and for democracy. Or they simply had to do it to survive. Sometimes, Bren, you just have to do some pretty heavy shit."

"I know," Bren answered. There was no conviction in her voice. "But do you ever feel bad about…?" She couldn't complete her sentence.

"Yes. I do," Cary answered quietly. He looked away, averting Bren's eyes.

FRIDAY, APRIL 1, 2011

Breaking News stared at Cary as *The 11 O'Clock News* began. *College Student Killed on Campus* crept across the bottom of the television as Kimberly Teller appeared on the screen. She was sitting at KEHT's anchor desk, a rare event. For a nanosecond, the name "Anne Korman" flashed across the lower portion of the screen, incorrectly identifying her. A moment later, her correct name appeared. Cary did not catch the April Fool's Day joke. He was too tired for details.

"A college coed was found murdered in her University of Columbiana dormitory today," Kimberly reported. "Her body was found in a basement laundry room of Jonathan L. Siegel Hall. There are no suspects. Campus police have asked the Oakville Police Department to assist in the investigation. In other news today, a major traffic tie-up occurred during the afternoon commute when…"

Cary fell asleep.

SATURDAY, APRIL 2, 2011

Cary was still asleep in his gray Lazy-Boy when KEHT's *Saturday A.M. News* began. Weekend anchor Cassie Morales was seated next to meteorologist Trent Levine. Neither was smiling.

"We begin with the news of a fatal shooting in Columbiana City," Cassie began. "A thirty-four-year-old man was gunned down in the Uptown neighborhood late last night as he got into his car. Witnesses reported the victim had been celebrating his brother's birthday at The Pitcher. They also reported a black pickup truck cruised by the bar several times prior to the incident. Loud country music and homophobic slurs were reported coming from the vehicle. Investigators urge anyone with information to contact Columbiana City police."

Cary heard none of this.

Instead, he was awakened by the theme music of *Saturday A.M. News* as the program signed off. "Oh crap!" he grunted as he opened his eyes. *Why did I fall asleep in this damn chair? I feel like shit,* he thought. He closed his eyes. *No. Wait. I can't go back to sleep. I have a nine o'clock car servicing appointment.* Cary rose from his recliner, groaned, and tried to twist the stiffness out of his back. As he walked to the kitchen for coffee, Cary realized he had a busy day ahead. Several chores and errands had to be completed after the car servicing. *They better be done by eleven like they said. I've got too much to do.*

The car servicing was finished on time. Cary then darted from the bank, to the dry cleaner, to the pharmacy, and to the grocery store before he became aware something tragic had happened overnight. As he left the grocery store parking lot, he caught the end of a radio news report. All he heard, however, was "…shot in front of The Pitcher last night. He died at the scene." He learned more details, unexpected details, when he watched *The News @ 5.*

"The man shot last night outside The Pitcher, a small bar catering to a mixed but mostly gay clientele, has been identified as Derek Stone, a Metropolitan Community College history professor," announced anchor Marletta Gaines, a thirtyish, attractive, medium-complexioned African American.

"Oh, my god!" gasped Cary, as he bolted out of his chair.

"It is reported he was attending a birthday party for his brother," Marletta continued. "He leaves a wife, Karolyn, and two small children. Investigators ask anyone with information regarding this crime to contact Columbiana City police."

"Derek. It was Derek? Oh, my god! No." Cary felt the color disappear from his cheeks, his heart sink to his feet. "Derek," he repeated in disbelief. "You were celebrating your brother's birthday like the great family man you were." Unaware it was happening, tears silently rolled down Cary's cheeks. His knees weakened and he fell back into his chair. "Derek," he said again. "Professor Stone." He wiped his cheeks with the heels of his hands. "Why?" Cary took a shaky breath. "This is just plain wrong," he added as anger began to mix with disbelief.

Trent Levine now smiled from the television screen, a sunny weather map behind him.

"Damn," Cary suddenly spat. "Damn, damn, damn!"

SUNDAY, APRIL 3, 2011

Murdered U of C Student ID'd inched across the screen as KEHT weekend anchor Marletta Gaines began *The News @ 5"*

"The young woman found dead in the laundry room of a University of Columbiana dormitory has been identified as twenty-two-year-old Emily Westmoreland, a 2007 graduate of Columbiana City's Centennial High School," Marletta began. "She appeared to have been strangled. Westmoreland was senior class president at Centennial, as well as captain of the girls' soccer team. At the U of C, she was co-chairperson of the school's gay, lesbian, bisexual and transgender student group."

Cary sat up.

"Emily had volunteered many hours at Oakville's food bank, The Cupboard, and tutored elementary school students struggling with reading and writing. She was scheduled to graduate in June with a degree in Women's Studies," Marletta continued. "Police are following up on leads."

First, the Snakes explosion, Cary thought. *Now, Derek and this woman are murdered on the same weekend. This is no coincidence. They're related. They're either directly connected to Al Kirk, SAM, and their initiative campaign or inspired by it.* Cary sighed. *Well, Kirk promised us a war, a culture war. If that's what he wants, he'll get it. But he has not yet met the enemy.*

WEDNESDAY, APRIL 6, 2011

"This is The Noon News and I'm Lacey Powers," greeted the KEHT anchor as *Arrests Made in Emily Westmoreland Murder* crawled across the base of the television screen. Cary was standing in front of the set, aiming the remote control at it; he had been a moment away from clicking off the television and heading to the MetComm Campus. But the ticker's brief headline stopped him. He placed his briefcase on the floor, sat down on the edge of his recliner, and watched.

"Oakville police have arrested two people in the University of Columbiana murder of Emily Westmoreland," Lacey stated. "The two, Reva Hassam and her brother, Omar Hassam, are students at the college. Police credit another student, Rob McNamara, with providing the lead that led to the arrests. Kimberly Teller has Rob with her." A live shot of Kimberly standing in front of the university's wine-red brick student union building appeared. "Good afternoon, Kimberly."

"Good afternoon, Lacey," Kimberly responded. "Yes, I do have Rob McNamara here." The camera pulled back to include a shaggy-haired, unshaven young man. "Rob, what did you tell the police that was so vital in their finding these alleged killers?"

"Well, Emily and I are, I mean were, cochairmen of the GLBTQ group here. And Em got a note from a woman who wanted to meet her. She wanted to talk privately about coming out. That is not unusual. We get communications like that all the time. But it wasn't an email, text, or phone message. This note was typed on a computer, printed, and left in our box here in the student union building. In hindsight, now, I realize this made it untraceable. We don't even have a handwriting sample."

"What did the note say, Rob?"

"It was weird, Kimberly. The woman said she was a devout Muslim and thought she was a lesbian. She needed to talk to someone. But it had to be very secretive, she said, because other Muslims could not find out she was having this conversation. Especially her father and brother. She implied she was very scared of them. Well, Em and I totally understood her predicament. We even understood why the note was not signed. Well, we *thought* we understood. The woman insisted Em meet her alone in the laundry room in the dorm basement at one o'clock in the morning. That, we thought, was a bit extreme."

"Why did Emily go then?" Kimberly asked.

"Well, I didn't want her to go. But she felt this woman needed help. Em said the woman was not only scared as a possible lesbian, but as a woman. Em helped people, took care of people in need. She cared for people. Anyone who knew her knew that." Rob stopped. His eyes began to glisten. He turned away from the camera to compose himself. After a beat, he turned back toward Kimberly. "And this is what she got. For being nice."

"So how did you suspect it was the Hassams?"

"Oh, OK. So, I was with Em. I waited on the main floor in the TV room. Only I wasn't watching TV. I was looking out the window, thinking about stuff. Remember, it was one o'clock. It was dark outside and the courtyard was pretty quiet. After she'd been gone maybe ten minutes, I saw a short woman in a head scarf — you know, the kind that Muslim women wear that covers the head but not the face — and a man rush by. I recognized the woman because I had a class with her last quarter. And the man was very identifiable. He was tall and very thin. He was quite dark; I presumed an Arab. He had a very hard look about him. Intense."

"Did you know their names?"

"No. In fact, I didn't even make the connection at first. Then I thought, 'Oh, maybe that was the woman.' Then I realized that if a man was with her, she had been followed or caught. I expected Em to come upstairs at any minute and tell me what a disaster it had been. But ten minutes went by and she didn't come up. So I went down." Rob stopped.

"You found Emily's body, didn't you, Rob?"

"Yes," he answered with a shaky voice.

"You called the police."

Rob nodded.

"I know this has been really difficult for you," Kimberly said, "but we do appreciate your time and telling your very painful story. Back to you in the studio, Lacey."

Lacey reappeared on the screen. "We'll be right back," she said somberly.

Cary exhaled. *That bitch set up Emily*, he thought as he clicked off the television. He pounded the arm of his recliner, stood, picked up his briefcase, and walked to the door. "Damn!" he screamed, as he opened it.

SATURDAY, APRIL 9, 2011

Cary climbed out of bed, stepped into his slippers, and shuffled into the kitchen to make coffee. It was late enough, and therefore light enough, to do this task without turning on the overhead light. Task completed, he turned and headed toward the bathroom. He glimpsed the Greenpeace calendar hanging on the wall as he passed and stopped. *Oh, crap,* he thought. *It's my birthday.*

As he returned from the bathroom, Cary, knowing the coffee would not yet be ready, wandered into the living room. He gazed out the large front window and noticed a car parked in front of his house. *What's Jules doing here?* he thought as the doorbell rang.

"Open the door, Old Man!" Jules called from the porch as the bell chimed a second insistent time. "I know you're up. Let me in!"

Cary padded to the door, opened it, gawked at his friend on the porch, and asked, "What the hell are you doing here, Jules?"

"Celebrating your birthday, Old Man," she answered as she stepped into the living room holding a white paper bag. "I know you hate birthdays and like them to go unnoticed, so I'm acknowledging it low-key and quickly. I brought bagels and then I'll go and let you ignore the rest of the day. I hope you've made coffee."

"It should be done. Come into the kitchen."

As Cary took two thrift store mugs from the cupboard and poured the coffee, Jules grabbed a plate from a neighboring shelf and arranged four assorted bagels on it. She then laid a cheap, gaudy, diamond-like bauble on each. Cary, with the two full mugs securely in his hands, turned around to bring them to the table. "Oh, my," he said as he spied the decorated treats. "What is this?"

"Do you like my jewels?" Jules asked.

"Very much," he said as they sat down.

"So what do you have planned on this very important day that you want to ignore?"

"Nothing really," Cary answered. "I've thought about going to the memorial for Tom Sandberg, that Snakes victim. They scheduled it for his birthday, you know. And I thought since we were connected by birthday maybe I should go to honor him. But I won't know any of the people there and have no history with him, so maybe not."

Jules, as promised, left soon after finishing her bagels and coffee. Cary continued debating whether to attend the memorial and eventually opted not to go. Instead, he frittered away the day, having the low-key birthday he wanted. In fact, by the time the news came on at five, he had forgotten it was birthday.

Protesters Greet Mourners moved across the screen as *The News @ 5* began. Cary sat up in his recliner. Marletta Gaines faced him, sitting in the anchor chair. "Pickets surprised mourners at the memorial for local entertainer Tom Sandberg today," Marletta announced. "Cassie Morales stepped away from the news desk and was there. Good evening, Cassie. Who were these protesters?"

"Good evening, Marletta. Before I explain who they are, I should remind viewers who Tom Sandberg was," Cassie said from the driveway of Snakes' parking lot. "Tom was one of the victims of the Valentine's Day bombing at Snakes. He died several weeks after the explosion. Tom was a performer, an avant-garde female impersonator named Tamara Today, who frequently hosted and performed in events at Snakes, as he was on Valentine's Day. His friends scheduled his memorial for today because it would have been his thirtieth birthday. This was the first event at Snakes since the bombing. The repaired wall and men's restroom were completed just days ago."

"Mourners who began arriving early this afternoon were surprised to find picketers blocking the driveway into the club's parking lot," Cassie continued. The camera swung to the picketers many of whom were marching back and forth across the driveway, chanting, and holding signs condemning homosexuals and homosexuality. Others prayed. "As you can hear, Marletta, the volume of their chants is rather disruptive. And I would be remiss, if I did not report that the chants contained frequent, vulgar, homophobic slurs." The camera swung back to Cassie. "Attendees of the memorial were forced to park on the street and walk through the loud, disruptive picketers. Words were exchanged. Confrontations did occur. But there was no physical violence."

"Were police present, Cassie?" Marletta asked.

"Yes, they were. In fact, one is here now." Cassie walked toward a policeman stationed several yards away from the protesters. "This is Officer Jay Vincent," she said as she reached him. "How did things go today, Officer Vincent?"

"Basically very well. There were a few moments I thought could have escalated," he said, "but they didn't. That was largely, I might add, because of the restrained behavior of the mourners. When asked by another officer or myself to do something, they responded appropriately. I can't say that was as true for the protesters who repeatedly moved into the street hampering traffic and putting themselves and others at risk."

"Thank you, Officer," Cassie said. "We appreciate your time."

From the studio, Marletta asked, "Where did the protesters come from, Cassie?"

"Well, oddly enough, Marletta, they're not from the United States. They came from Southern Ontario, Canada. According to their leader, Phil Fredericks, they come from a small town, Edenot, just across the border from Detroit. They formed a caravan and drove the considerable distance to get here, to get to Columbiana City."

"Who do they represent?"

"They are from the Church of God's Love, Marletta. Phil Fredericks is its minister and family head. These protesters are all from the Fredericks Family. The church essentially consists of one large family."

"How many of the Fredericks Family are picketing? And, just as important, how many people attended the memorial?"

"There were easily four hundred friends and family here to remember Tom. Most of them have gone now," Cassie answered. "As for the protesters, I counted twenty-three, some of whom are young children, and they're still here. I was told they are staying to confront patrons when they arrive for the bar's reopening tonight." Just as Cassie said that, a young boy, perhaps ten years old, stepped into the camera's range and yelled, "God hates queers!"

Unflustered, Cassie calmly said, "That is sort of typical of what has been going on at Snakes today, Marletta. I'll be here to give an update at 11:00."

"Thank you, Cassie."

The news set appeared. Marletta looked somewhat rattled, perhaps by the boy's comment. "We'll be right back," she said quietly.

When they returned, the anchorwoman announced that a flurry of activity had occurred at the entry to the Snakes parking lot since their last report. As Marletta said, "Cassie, can you tell us what's happening?" the reporter appeared on the screen, sidestepping Frederick Family protesters as they scurried to pack their signs and load the large group into several cars and minibuses.

"Yes, Marletta," Cassie said. "A young woman just told me that her father, Phil Frederick, had received a message from God and they were to leave immediately. She did not know why. But, as you can see, the protesting Frederick Family is leaving. That would mean, I assume, they won't be here later tonight to confront club patrons as they arrive. That is all for now, Marletta. Back to you in the studio."

SUNDAY, APRIL 10, 2011

Cary tuned into the morning news a few minutes late and missed the beginning of the lead story. But he knew something important had happened overnight as soon as he saw the image on the screen. Cassie Morales was standing on the street next to the driveway leading into Snakes' parking lot. In the background, Cary could see what appeared to be several burnt-out cars parked along the curb.fr Yellow crime tape cordoned off the damaged cars. Cassie was interviewing a young man in a tight, hot pink T-shirt. Chest-high, across the shirt's front was the word "SnakeStaff." The "t" was shaped like a staff. Serpents entwined the two esses. At the bottom of the screen, the man was identified as "Stan Raymond, Snakes Security."

"…and you recognized them?" Cassie asked.

"Yes, Cassie. Immediately," the muscular bouncer answered. "They had on fake moustaches and one had a wide-brimmed hat that I think was to hide his face. The other had his hood up covering his hair. That in itself made them look suspicious. But I recognized their sweatshirts. They were the same ones they had been wearing while picketing this afternoon."

"So, what did you do, Stan?"

"Well, I radioed for backup before these two suspicious-looking guys even got to the head of the line. When they got to me, I checked their IDs. The Canadian IDs they had said their names were Peter Trudeau and Timothy Horton and that they were from Halifax, Nova Scotia. Now, Cassie," and Stan snorted a short laugh, "I've been to Canada. I know that Tim Horton's is a restaurant chain. I told them we wouldn't accept their IDs. I think that is when my backups, Carlos and Tisha, showed up. The two guys gave Carlos and Tisha the once-over and one of them asked why I wouldn't accept their IDs. I asked them why they'd been picketing here earlier in the day and they bolted. I wish we had called the police, but they hadn't really done anything illegal yet. Except, maybe make really bad fake Canadian IDs."

"And less than twenty minutes later, Marletta," Cassie said, turning to the camera, "the three cars on the street were torched. All three cars belong to people who had been at Snakes last night."

"Have these two suspicious characters been linked to the damage done to the cars?" the anchor woman asked.

"Police are investigating, Marletta. They are asking that question and they are asking what the duo's intentions were had they gotten inside Snakes. Hopefully, police will have some answers for us at *The News @ 5*."

The only new information police had by five o'clock regarding the torched cars, however, was that U.S. border patrol agents had confirmed the Frederick Family had crossed back into Canada just after midnight. But they could not confirm if the two men with questionable IDs were with them. That would have been quite unlikely since they were at the bar near midnight. Because that story had no major developments, the news began instead with an important development from a previous story.

Columbiana City's Number One News Source--KEHT Channel 8--April 10, 2011 flowed across the television screen. It was followed by *Suspects in College Professor's Murder Arrested*. "I'm Mac Hines and this is *The News @ 5*," the stony-faced anchor said.

"Three Braxton men were arrested today for the April 1st shooting of local history professor Derek Strong. Travis Gunderson, 21, his brother Ian Gunderson, 19, and Lyle Henshaw, 19, were booked into Pratt County Jail Saturday. The trio was arrested in a Braxton church parking lot where police had received a tip they might be found. When police arrived, they observed the older Gunderson transferring two cases of beer from his truck to the Henshaw car. At nineteen, Henshaw is a minor. Details are being arranged with local police to have them moved to Columbiana City. Kimberly Teller is at The Pitcher, across the street from where the shooting occurred. Good evening, Kimberly."

"Good evening, Mac." The reporter appeared on screen with an older man. "I'm with The Pitcher owner Lech Orvicz," she said. "It was the bar's security cameras that helped police identify and capture Prof. Strong's alleged killers."

"Yes, I put cameras up outside after Snakes bomb," Orvicz explained in a thick Polish accent. It was clear he struggled with English. "One was on corner and other by door. So police look at video and see truck my customers say go by bar many times. License was hard to see, detective tells me, because it was dark. But they make picture better. And that camera," Orvicz said, pointing to the door, "makes license clear. They also see large sticker BHS on back window of truck. Yes. Lech Orvicz maybe not speak English good but I am smart businessman and good helping American." He smiled proudly.

"On that positive note," Kimberly ended, "we return to the studio and you, Mac."

Cary stared at the television. *Braxton,* he thought. *That's where Kayo and Dan spent all those years.*

MONDAY, APRIL 11, 2011

"Police have tentatively identified the two persons of interest in the car torching near Snakes late Saturday night," announced Mac Hines well into *The News @ 5.* "Based on our film capturing the two men as they picketed Saturday's memorial and Snakes' security cameras, police believe the two men are Christian Frederick, 23, and his cousin Dolph Hiller, 21. Police also confirm that the two suspects crossed into Canada late last night using valid passports, not the allegedly false IDs they tried to use at the dance club. Police urge any witnesses to the cars being torched to step forward. Without witnesses, they say, no charges can be made and, therefore, no request for extradition can be filed."

MONDAY, MAY 30, 2011

Cary's eyes flickered open. He looked at the clock on the bedside night stand. It was nearly ten o'clock in the morning. He did not move. *Thank god it's Memorial Day,* he thought, *and I don't have to get up.* He dozed off again.

When he awoke after noon, Cary's mind danced from thought to thought in a stream-of-consciousness conga line: *Got to check with Kayo and Jules about locations…The last six weeks have really been quiet…No news from SAM…Did I finish recording those grades?…I should have bought gas before the prices went up for the holiday…Did Kayo ever say what Dan's last name was?…Call Nick. Leave a message if he won't pick up…And, God, please make him pick up…I sure hope those three Braxton bastards are having a good time in jail.*

Cary's entire afternoon was as disjointed as his thoughts. After he got up and showered, he shaved. An hour later, he realized he'd only shaved one side of his face. When he went outside to do some weeding, he took only one glove and the broken spade he had intended to throw out last summer. After he finished his yard work, Cary went inside, made himself some coffee and dropped his favorite coffee mug, the one his son Nick had given him as a child for Father's Day, shattering it. When he decided he wanted Piece-A-Pizza for dinner, he drove off without his wallet and driver's license.

Even KEHT's news programming was disorganized. *The News @ 5* was seen at six thirty due to special Memorial Day programming. When it was finally aired, however, it got Cary's attention.

Memorial Day 2011 slid across the screen. *Picnics, BBQs, Families, Travel, Recreation, Fun, and the News* followed as Marletta Gaines appeared. "This is a delayed version of *The News @ 5* and I'm Marletta Gaines. We start with a picnic held today by the supporters of the initiative to stop gay marriage. Save America's Marriages met today at Riverside Park."

Footage from earlier in the day appeared on the screen. Al Kirk, picnicking in slacks and a long sleeve dress shirt and a patriotically striped tie, was addressing several hundred supporters. Two American flags were draped behind him. Next to him stood State Senator Mike Malone wearing a red, white, and blue "America: Love It or Leave It!" T-shirt.

"We are pleased to announce," Kirk said, "that we have collected the required number of signatures to qualify for the November ballot." Before he had finished the sentence, the crowd erupted in wild cheering. When the celebrating had quieted, Kirk continued. "We have nearly 200,000 signatures, well beyond the required 163,000." There was more cheering. Handheld flags were waved. "So, my friends, we will be on the ballot in November and we will win!" The crowd roared. "I predict the end of the gay agenda is near," Kirk said with confidence. The crowd's thunderous reply teetered on hysteria. Cary sighed.

"And now State Senator Malone has something to say," Kirk went on as the roar became hushed excitement.

"Hello, my fellow Columbianans," Malone greeted loudly. "Tomorrow, we will be delivering boxes of signed initiatives to the Secretary of State's office in Stover to be validated. We are well over the number of signatures needed and far ahead of the deadline. We are forming a caravan and will be leaving the Columbiana City Baptist Church parking lot at nine thirty. Join us!"

Cary sighed again. *As if today hasn't been bad enough,* he thought.

TUESDAY, MAY 31, 2011

Lacey Powers was reporting on an early morning apartment complex fire in the outskirts of Columbiana City on *NoonNews8* when the headline first progressed across the lower portion of the television screen. *Anti-Gay Marriage Signatures Delivered to Sec. of State* it read.

As promised, thought Cary.

"And now to the state capital where Kimberly Teller reports from the Secretary of State's office," Lacey announced. "Good afternoon, Kimberly," she said, as the familiar reporter came into view. She was standing in the hallway of the stately, old office building. Marble walls and dark oak wood surrounded her. A doorway to her rear had "Office of the Secretary of State" stenciled on it.

"Good afternoon, Lacey," Kimberly greeted. "Leaders of Save America's Marriages just delivered several boxes containing, according to their estimate, nearly 200,000 signatures asking voters to overturn the law passed by the state legislature and signed by Gov. Oleson that would allow same-sex couples to marry beginning January 1, 2012." Live coverage from inside the office appeared with Kimberly performing a voice-over. The camera moved from a distant shot far down the office's long counter to a close-up of SAM's boxes stacked on a pushcart to a group shot of Al Kirk, Sandi Iglesias, and Sen. Malone presenting the initiatives to a representative of the office. "The signatures will be counted and verified here," Kimberly explained, "as will those of other initiatives that are turned in. Those making the ballot will be announced on July 5. Back to you, Lacey."

Cary gulped the last of his coffee, shut off the television, and left for his first class. Midway through the class he realized he had left at home a folder he needed for his evening class. He went home, found the folder, thumbed through the just-delivered mail, and perused the latest University of Hawaii alumni magazine. When he finished, Cary realized it was time for *The News @ 5*. He flipped on the broadcast to hear any updated information regarding the initiative.

By the time *The News @ 5* aired, an interview with Sen. Malone had been added to the report. "We do not hate gay people," he said. "We love them. But we are against their demeaning our marriages, the real marriages of millions of

Columbianans, both past and present." Gay marriage advocate Davis Wells was also interviewed. He repeated the tepid, politically correct comments he had made in February when the initiative was filed, welcoming "the opportunity to educate the good citizens of Columbiana about the issue and looking forward to a campaign that would be run on the high road."

"You and your fucking 'high road,'" grunted Cary. He shut off the television and headed back to campus.

SATURDAY, JUNE 4, 2011

Breaking News! Two Dead in Church Explosion raced with urgency across the television screen as *The News @ 5* began. A beautiful, blonde, angelic-looking woman sat in the weekend anchor chair. "I'm Grace Balfour," she said.

Cary did not notice that the anchorwoman was new, unfamiliar to KEHT's audience. He did not even hear her say her name. He was focused on the breaking news story.

"An explosion ripped through a small church killing two in the Southwestern Columbiana farm community of Slayton today," read the new anchor. "The explosion occurred just as a wedding was to begin at the First Evangelical Church of God. The minister, Rev. Paul Ferris, and the bride, Natalie Vickers, died at the scene. The groom, Jesse Ryan, received serious eye injuries and may be blinded. Several other members of the wedding party were also injured. All have been transported to University Hospital in Oakville. It appears the explosion occurred when Rev. Ferris turned on his microphone, witnesses said. Ferris is a known outspoken opponent of gay marriage and gay rights. Local police are investigating."

Cary sat back. "OK," he said with satisfaction as he sank into his recliner.

MONDAY, JUNE 13, 2011

Breaking News! Senator's Wife, Son Die in Mystery Car Fire exploded onto the television screen at 11:58 a.m. as a teaser to *NoonNews8*. Then two minutes of commercials and promos delayed the reporting of the urgent headline's details.

"The wife and son of State Sen. Mike Malone were killed this morning when their car exploded in their garage," Lacey Powers said. "We go to the scene and Kimberly Teller. Good afternoon, Kimberly."

"Good afternoon, Lacey," Kimberly responded from the sidewalk in front of a modern suburban home. There was obvious fire damage to its garage and an adjacent section of the house. "Mrs. Malone was taking nine-year-old Seth to the first day of camp, according to the senator, when the explosion occurred," Kimberly reported. "Investigators suspect the blast was triggered when Mrs. Malone turned the key in the ignition. Ruth Malone was thirty-nine years old. The explosion, as you can see, set fire to the garage and part of the Malones' Rolling Hills home. Sen. Malone was at home at the time of the explosion, but was at the opposite end of the house. He is with relatives."

"How tragic," Lacey commented. "Do investigators have any leads?"

"They have not reported any."

"Do they think the senator's role in the anti-gay marriage initiative could have played a part in this?"

"They are not counting anything out, Lacey. Back to you."

Cary sat back. "OK," he said with even more satisfaction than he felt when he heard the report of the June 4 church bombing. He sank relieved into his recliner.

THURSDAY, JUNE 16, 2011

Leads, No Suspects in Bombings scrolled across the screen repeatedly throughout the early minutes of the broadcast. But *The 11 O'Clock News* did not cover the story until 11:11.

"Police have found a small wrench with a 'CFD' insignia on it at the location where two people died in a church explosion Saturday," Mac Hines announced. Two Slayton residents told investigators they noticed a car with Illinois license plates in the church parking lot early Saturday morning. Both say they assumed its owner was here for Saturday's wedding. Police are asking anyone who may have taken a picture of the car or written down its license to contact either Slayton police or the state patrol.

"Meanwhile, fire marshals in Rolling Hills," Mac continued, "have determined the explosion that killed the wife and son of State Sen. Mike Malone on Monday was deliberately set. Evidence of tampered wires in the ignition and the use of accelerant were found, authorities reported. A crumpled plastic Home Depot bag also was found outside the garage. Investigators, however, have no leads." Mac paused a beat. "We'll be right back," he said.

"No, you won't," Cary retorted as he clicked off the television, rose from his recliner, and headed for bed.

SATURDAY, JUNE 18, 2011

It was 7:10 when Marletta Gaines interrupted Meteorologist Trent Levine during *Saturday A.M. News.* "We have breaking news," interrupted Marletta. "Faith's Flowers, located in Old Town, was broken into and vandalized overnight. According to police reports, the shop's entire inventory, including refrigerated floral arrangements for weddings today, was ruined. Flowers throughout the shop were found strewn on the floor, trampled and sprayed with a chemical rendering them useless. Owners Faith and Larry McWhorter report the damage was discovered by a staff member who arrived at five o'clock to finalize three large arrangements for weddings today. The staff member also reported finding a note typed on shocking pink paper that said, 'If we can't marry, no one can!' Police are investigating.

"The McWhorters and their staff are scrambling to find replacement flowers to salvage today's ceremonies. Hopefully, they will be successful and we can have a happy ending to this story." Marletta paused and appeared to be listening to someone speaking in her earpiece. "And we hope to have a camera crew at one of those weddings. OK. Back to you and the weather, Trent."

Kayo chuckled. *That sounds so Act Up*, he thought.

SUNDAY, JUNE 26, 2011

Columbiana City's Number One News Source--KEHT Channel 8--June 26, 2011 paraded across Cary's television as *The News @ 5* began. There was no alarming

"Breaking News!" alert, no teaser headline. It was, news-wise, a pretty boring day in Columbiana. Except that it was Gay Pride Day.

"The region's annual Gay Pride Parade drew an estimated crowd of forty thousand people today," anchor Cassie Morales said, as a large rainbow flag filled the screen. "The parade celebrated victories won in the gay rights movement, including February's passage of the gay marriage act, as well as accomplishments of individual gay, lesbian, bisexual, and transgender people through history. The day's theme 'One. Won.' seemed to reflect the unity of the day, and the symbolic unity of marriage, a topic that was on everyone's mind with the possibility of a November initiative rescinding the law."

As Cassie spoke, video ran showing the diversity of the participants in the parade and along the route. Sports groups demonstrated their sport as they marched; even the local gay swim club "swam" on foot. Employee and union organizations chanted as they walked. Drag queens entertained from flatbed trucks converted into floats. Gay and lesbian parents strolled with their children. Men in leather smiled and waved in a manner that contrasted with their overly masculine appearance. Straight allies from local churches paraded by carrying supportive signs. Gay, lesbian, bi, and transgender youth brought their joy and energy. Supportive politicians glad-handed parade-goers, hoping their support would be returned.

"But not all onlookers were celebrating," Cassie continued. "Members of Save America's Marriages stood along the parade route and in Riverside Park where it ended." The video showed an elderly couple dressed as the farm couple in Grant Wood's iconic painting *American Gothic*. The man held a sign saying, "Adam & Eve, Not Adam & Steve." The woman carried a placard boasting, "45 Years of Real Marriage." The picture returned to Cassie at the anchor desk. "There were a few confrontations along the route, police reported, but none were physical, and no arrests were made."

But by *The 11 O'Clock News*, the story had changed. *Violence at Gay Pride Event* dashed across the bottom of KEHT's logo as the broadcast began. "I'm Cassie Morales. After an apparent incident-free Gay Pride Day, things took a turn for the worse this evening. Kimberly Teller is at Riverside Park." Kimberly appeared on screen. "Can you tell us what happened there, Kimberly?"

"Yes, Cassie. A fundraiser for No on Discrimination, the group formed to counter Save America's Marriages' initiative if gay marriage is on the November ballot, was being held at the concert shell," Kimberly explained as she walked around the scene. "A number of musical groups and drag performers were entertaining a crowd of several hundred when four young men began running through the crowd yelling, shoving, pushing, and punching spectators. A few minor injuries were reported. The attack, it appears, was planned as a diversion because backstage, where entertainers awaited their turn to perform, another individual jumped a drag performer and attempted to strangle him. The performer, Hannah Mae DeLube, had stepped away from the other performers and was rehearsing his number in a shadowy area behind the concert shell, when someone blindsided him and began violently choking him. The assailant, however, must not have known that Hannah Mae is a trained self-defense instructor. Within a moment, the assailant was on the ground being held by Hannah Mae and two other performers who had heard the commotion and rushed over. Two of the individuals who attacked the audience also were detained by members of the crowd until police arrived. The three, all high school students, were arrested."

"Well," Cassie said, "that certainly was not a positive way to end an otherwise pleasant celebration. And one of the reasons it was so pleasant was the weather. When we return, Trent Levine will tell us if this weather will continue."

"Who are those jackasses?" Cary asked the television, as he shut it off. "I'll have to call Adam Shapiro in the morning to see what he can dig up."

MONDAY, JUNE 27, 2011

Halt to Violence Urged was the cryptic headline flowing across Cary's television screen as *The 11 O'Clock News* began. Mac Hines, sitting at the anchor desk, explained. "A hastily organized press conference called by Columbiana City Police Chief Philip Gerard was held this afternoon to urge supporters on both sides of the gay marriage debate to refrain from using violent tactics," Hines said. "He was joined by Davis Wells, chairman of No on Discrimination, Father

Shamus O'Reilly of the Catholic Archdiocese of Columbiana, and Rabbi Sarah Maimon of Congregation Beth Israel."

The picture morphed from the anchor live to video of Rabbi Maimon standing behind a bank of microphones. "There have been several instances of violence throughout our beautiful state over the past few months and they have one common denominator," the rabbi said. "The victims all have been connected in some way to the battle over gay marriage. This must stop. Three people died needlessly at Snakes in February. Smoke bombs were set as representatives of Save America's Marriages spoke in Stover. Signature gatherers have been harassed. A leader of a gay student organization was killed at the University of Columbiana. A local college professor was gunned down outside a gay bar. Two people died in a bombing of a wedding at a small church in a peaceful farming town. The wife and son of a state senator murdered. A beautiful florist shop vandalized. And last night, a concert was ruined by several assaults and what appears to be an attempted murder. We strongly urge leaders on both sides of the issue to take a stand *now* to stop this violence."

Rabbi Maimon handed the microphone to the police chief. "As for the high school boys responsible for last night's assaults, they are being held at the juvenile detention center. We are not naming them as they are minors."

Mac Hines reappeared. "We reached out to Save America's Marriages to ask why they were not represented at the press conference and received this statement from cochairman Sandi Iglesias. 'While we do not condone violence, we strongly resent the implication that SAM has been involved in any of the recent incidents and we find the suggestion ludicrous that SAM has inspired and encouraged others to act violently. We have not had a role in any criminal behavior. We only wish the leaders of NOD could say the same thing.'" Mac paused. "It is not clear, we should state, if the rabbi's statement implied or suggested SAM had played a role in or was responsible for any of the incidents listed." The screen darkened for a moment. KEHT went to a commercial break.

Cary had not heard this report. He did not see any of *The 11 O'Clock News*. He had left his house just before the news began, forgetting to turn off the television.

TUESDAY, JUNE 28, 2011

Columbiana City's Number One News Source--KEHT Channel 8--June 28, 2011 streamed across Cary's television screen below the logo for *NoonNews8* as the program's tension-filled theme played. Lacey Powers appeared. She quickly cut to an unfamiliar male reporter covering a jackknifed semi blocking the interstate just outside Columbiana City's southern boundary. "Who cares?" Cary yelled with frustration at the television. Then Lacey began a report that did capture his attention, the story for which he had been waiting.

"The mother of one of the boys charged with the assaults on spectators at a No on Discrimination fundraising concert held Sunday at Riverside Park was found dead in her bed this morning," Lacey announced. "The cause appears to be carbon monoxide poisoning. Her estranged husband found the body when he came to pick her up. They were scheduled to visit their son who is being held at the juvenile detention center. Because the son is a minor, police will not release either his or his mother's name. Investigators have identified a point through which the carbon monoxide may have entered the woman's bedroom. They also have a note that was taped to the home's front door. The contents of the note were not released."

That's what you get for failing to raise your kid right, Cary thought as he silenced the television and headed to work.

MONDAY, JULY 4, 2011

With graphics of fireworks behind it, the logo for *The News @ 5* burst on to the screen. The ticker running below it simply said *Happy Birthday, America — Happy 4th of July*. Marletta Gaines appeared at the anchor desk wearing a white blouse with a red, white, and blue stars and stripes scarf around her neck. Dangling from her earlobes were tiny stars in the same three colors.

"To those not picnicking or at a barbecue right now, welcome," she greeted viewers. "Today is the Fourth of July. We remind everyone to be careful with all fireworks and firecrackers tonight. The region has already had several fireworks-related mishaps. The worst incident occurred in East Stover last night during the town's annual Pre-4 Celebration when, according to fire officials, an errant firework set Holy Trinity Church ablaze burning the wooden structure to the ground."

Cary stared unfocused at the screen, distracted by the jarring explosions of nearby firecrackers. As a strikingly loud one rattled Cary's house, his television screen flashed what was assumed to be the burnt remnants of the East Stover church. But the film looked grainy, dated, and somehow familiar. "What the hell!" Cary spat. "That was the ROTC building we bombed." The momentary image was gone. He pounded the heels of his hands on his temples to clear his head. "Where'd that come from? Was that stock footage they use for fires?" He blinked his eyes and then opened them wider to erase the startling, unexpected image and refocus on Marletta's report. Footage of Holy Trinity Church's charred skeleton appeared on the screen. All that remained of a wooden sign on its lawn identifying the church were the letters "Ho...T...."

The news anchor continued. "The church's minister, Rev. Tim Shayne immediately went online blaming 'homosexuals and the supporters of their agenda.'" Marletta turned to the weather map. "So, Trent, what will the weather be like for tonight's fireworks?"

"Very Christian, Reverend," Cary mumbled cynically. "Like we'd be responsible for something like that." And then he rubbed his eyes and laughed.

TUESDAY, JULY 5, 2011

It was 5:06 p.m. when Cary raced into his house. He quickly turned on his television to watch *The News @ 5* to find out which initiatives had qualified for November's election.

"... and besides the gay marriage initiative," Mac Hines was saying, "only two others qualified for the ballot. One bans pit bulls as pets and the other requires high school athletic coaches to be certified teachers. Failing to receive the necessary signatures were initiatives to raise the gas tax and to ban online gambling in the state."

We're on the ballot. What a surprise, Cary thought sarcastically. *The war goes on.*

SUNDAY, JULY 10, 2011

Pro 614 Emails Hacked moved across the screen at the end of several other teasers as KEHT's *The News @ 5* began. Cary sat up in his recliner, his curiosity piqued. "It is Sunday, July 10," began anchor Marletta Gaines. Cary leaned forward. The anchor, however, did not report on the email hacking until twelve minutes into the newscast.

"There are new developments in the campaign to outlaw same-sex marriage," Marletta announced. "The church computers of Save America's Marriages Campaign Cochairman Rev. Al Kirk, were hacked overnight. Rev. Kirk made the discovery this morning when he arrived at his church, The Hope Tabernacle Temple."

Kirk appeared on the screen. "The moment I turned on my computer I knew something was wrong," he said. "I had received hundreds of new emails overnight and I realized most came from my church members. All the emails were the same. They said in bold letters 'Vote No on Initiative 614.' That is the exact opposite of what we stand for, what Save America's Marriages stands for."

"What do you think happened, Rev. Kirk?" an off-camera voice asked.

"Well, it took me a moment, and then I realized our weekly newsletter — it's just a page — was programmed to be sent at midnight. It had been hacked. The newsletter, which is emailed to all parishioners, had been infected. Once our members received it, their contact lists got infected too. Apparently, it triggered automatic responses from anyone who received it to the original sender, me. Who knows how many other email contact lists have been compromised?"

"Do you know who would have done this?" the off-camera voice asked.

"Well," Kirk replied testily, "who do you think? Who has the motive? The homosexuals. Their agenda has always been to gain special rights and interfere with Christians' right to freedom of religion."

Marletta Gaines appeared again on screen. "No on Discrimination Chairman Davis Wells responded, "We had nothing to do with this illegal activity. We have said from the beginning that we would be running a campaign on the high road."

Cary looked puzzled. *Bren?* he thought.

FRIDAY, JULY 15, 2011

Survey Shows Mixed Results in Initiative Races read the streaming headline as KEHT's *NoonNews8* began. "Results of a statewide survey on the three initiatives on November's ballot were released just minutes ago by McGraw-Pitts research," Lacey Powers said, beginning the news.

"Initiative 614, the anti-gay marriage initiative would be approved 53 to 39 percent, if the election were held today. Eight percent remain undecided. Those figures are quite similar to a March survey's findings, although the 'undecided' number has grown slightly. The pit bull measure, Initiative 619, is a virtual dead heat with 42 percent in favor of banning the dogs as pets and 41 percent saying 'no.' Seventeen percent are undecided. Initiative 612, requiring high school coaches to have teaching degrees appears headed to defeat with a whopping 63 percent opposed."

Not looking good, Cary thought, as he shut off the set and headed to campus.

SATURDAY, JULY 23, 2011

Body Found in Playas' Parking Lot drifted across the bottom of Cary's television screen as *The News @ 5* began. Mac Hines sat at the anchor desk, a rarity on weekends.

"A man's body was found in the parking lot of popular singles bar Playas this morning," the anchorman said. "It was discovered by a member of the custodial crew. Cassie Morales is at the scene. "Good evening, Cassie. What can you tell us about this discovery?"

"Good evening, Mac. The body of the twenty-three-year-old man was found by a Playas employee when he arrived to clean up the bar," Cassie reported. "He told me he pulled into the Playas' parking lot just after eight this morning, saw the victim's pickup truck parked by itself near the lot's far end, and investigated. That is when he discovered the body lying across the vehicle's bench seat."

"Was foul play involved?" Mac asked.

"Police are not releasing details until the family has been notified. The pickup truck bears California plates. Back to you in the studio, Mac."

MONDAY, JULY 25, 2011

Cary missed the first several minutes of *The News @ 5*. By the time he tuned in, anchor Marletta Gaines was reporting developments and details in Saturday's Playas' parking lot discovery.

"…was a June graduate of UCLA, where he majored in Business Administration. He had just moved here last week and was to start a job in the telecommunications industry today. Gibson is survived by his parents and two siblings." Marletta paused a moment. "Playas' security cameras captured Gibson and a woman as they left the club."

A still shot from the security video show the couple in the well-lit Playas' entry. Gibson has shoulder-length blond hair. He is wearing board shorts with a white muscle shirt with a Playboy bunny logo. The slender woman is wearing a white blouse and dark skirt. The blouse is unbuttoned enough to expose red lace on her bra. She is also wearing lace trimmed red gloves. Her straight, dark hair falls halfway down her back.

Marletta reappeared on the screen. "Anyone with information, please contact Columbiana City Police," she added.

TUESDAY, JULY 26, 2011

Gruesome Details Emerge in Playas Murder scrolled across Cary's television, as *The 11:00 O'Clock News* began. It caught Cary's attention.

"Police have released details of this weekend's apparent murder in the Playas' parking lot. Pete Gibson's body was found in his pickup truck Saturday morning," anchor Mac Hines reported. "We warn you details may not be suitable for all viewers."

Video of a police spokesperson speaking to a bank of microphones appeared on screen. "Mr. Gibson was stabbed in the heart and the throat," the man said. Superimposed across his chest was the identification "Sgt. Luke Devanny, Columbiana City Police." "His blood-soaked white muscle shirt was pushed up exposing his stomach and his pants were at his ankles. The end of his penis had been severed. Considerable blood covered the vehicle's front seat and foot well. Written on Gibson's stomach in red lipstick was the name Lola. Across the gray dashboard, scrawled in the same red lipstick, was the phrase "4 Shame, 4 Shane." Police would like to talk with the woman seen leaving Playas with Pete Gibson late Friday night and any witnesses who may have seen or heard something suspicious in the bar or parking lot that night."

Mac Hines reappeared. "Twenty-three-year-old Pete Gibson had been president of his college fraternity at UCLA, an assistant Boy Scout leader, and part-time surfing instructor. He leaves behind his siblings Kara and Tyler Gibson and their adoptive dads, David Fletcher and Jim Aaron."

THURSDAY, JULY 28, 2011

Cary raised his coffee mug to his lips and sipped. With caution, he placed the mug on a pile of magazines on the cluttered end table next to his recliner. He then gripped the chair's arm, and pushed back. Comfortably reclined, he grabbed the television remote and clicked. *The Morning News* had just begun.

"A city sanitation worker has discovered what may be evidence related to last weekend's Playas' parking lot murder," Lacey Powers said. "He found a bag-like purse in an apartment building yard waste bin near Playas. It contained a woman's long black wig, a blood splattered woman's white blouse and black skirt, a red lipstick tube, red lacey gloves, and a bloodied knife. The worker realized his discovery could be related to the Playas murder and called police. Police have turned the find over to forensic experts. They expect results in a week or so."

SUNDAY, AUGUST 7, 2011

Kayo broke through the brittle, brown summer-dried vegetation leading to The Pub and was surprised to find Cary sitting on the ground staring in his direction with a look that communicated, "Now, who the fuck is this?"

"Hi. What are you doing here?" Kayo asked.

"Thinking. I was about to ask you the same thing."

"Thinking about what?"

"Lots of stuff, Kayo. Lots of stuff."

"Like?" Kayo asked, as he sat down next to Cary.

Cary played with a tuft of dried grass for a moment. Then he retied the laces of one of his navy blue New Balance tennis shoes even though they were not loose. Kayo watched his friend's evasive behavior with curiosity.

"Like," Cary finally responded, "like…oh shit, I don't even know how to say this, ask this. Never mind."

"What? Are you OK, man? Are you in some kind of trouble?"

"Yeah. I'm OK. No, I'm not in trouble. It's just…Kayo, remember when I told you how you looked at Ben Lieber back when we all were raisin' hell? When the pot caused you to let your guard down?"

"Yeah."

"Well, why didn't you ever look at me that way? There. I said it."

"Why didn't I look at you the way I looked at Ben, even though I was try-ing desperately to hide my feelings for Ben?" Kayo paused to form an answer to a question he had never considered. "Because," he said, "you're Cary and he's Ben. He affected me in a way I'd never felt before. I really didn't understand it. The physical part. I didn't know how to interpret it. But you, man? You're my brother. I love you as a brother, man. Why are you even asking this?"

Cary swallowed. "Because I've always wondered what would have happened if you had looked at me that way and I'd picked up on it and we were high and alone and horny, which all guys in their twenties are all the time?"

"Are you telling me you are gay, Cary?"

"No. I'm just wondering about all the what ifs in my life? What if we had done something? What would it have been? Would I have liked it? If I didn't, if it freaked me out, would our friendship have survived? Or if I did like it, would we have become a couple? Would the thirty-five years we didn't see or hear from one another been erased?"

Kayo looked pensive for a moment. "OK. Here's what probably would have happened," Kayo theorized. "If we had had some kind of sex, since you are not gay, it would have been weird and awkward for you. It would have been an experiment, an experience. I would have probably had an *aha* moment and thought, 'Oh, now I get it! This is who I am.'" Kayo paused. "But I don't think it would have even happened, because I really wasn't ready for it yet and, like I said, I didn't see you that way. You didn't turn me on. As close as we were, as much as I cared for you, man, you weren't Ben Lieber."

"I suppose you're right." Cary said with resignation. He looked at Kayo. "So, what you felt for Dan was like your feelings for Ben?"

"Yes."

"OK. I think I get it." Cary sat up, looked toward the wall of wild shrubs blocking the river view, and turned to face Kayo again. "Hey, why are you here anyway?"

"Oh, I just came to smoke this joint a neighbor gave me for watering her plants while she was away," he answered as he reached into his deep blue aloha shirt pocket. "I'll share."

"Alright." Cary watched Kayo light the joint with a black Bic lighter he had pulled from his pants pocket. Kayo took a long drag and handed the joint to Cary.

Kayo exhaled. "So it's my turn. I have a question for you," he said as Cary took a toke. "Why is the gay marriage issue so important to you? It isn't your battle. You don't have a dog in this fight, man. There are any number of other issues you could have gotten involved with, issues that impact you more. The environment. That damn war in Iraq. Big business's takeover of our political system."

Cary emptied his lungs. "I thought I told you back at Starbuck's in February." He passed the joint to Kayo. "I thought you were gay. You disappeared after prison. I figured you had come out and wanted to separate yourself from your past. Then, after AIDS had been around a few years, I thought you were dead." He motioned to Kayo, who was holding the joint in midair focused on Cary's words, to take a toke. Kayo raised the marijuana to his lips. "So," Cary continued, "I thought I should do this for you since you couldn't."

"For me?" Kayo said with surprise before he had a chance to inhale.

"Yeah. Because, like I said, you couldn't. But there was a second reason, man."

"What?" Kayo asked, and took another toke.

"Atonement. Atonement for my sins. My sins against you."

"What sins against me?"

Cary reached for the joint. "I was responsible for your going to prison, man." He looked down. "And I let you go alone. I should have stepped up."

Kayo stared at Cary who was still looking down. "Look at me, man," Kayo ordered. Cary slowly looked up. A lone tear rolled down his cheek.

"Cary, you are not responsible for what happened to me. I am. I got myself into prison. My decisions, my actions got me in prison. And as for stepping up, man, I would have done the same, if the roles had been reversed. You have no reason to feel responsible for what happened to me, no reason to feel guilt. Besides, if I hadn't gone to prison, I wouldn't have met Dan."

Cary smiled and took another puff of marijuana and exhaled. "That's enough for me." He turned his head and looked at his friend. "You know, Kayo, I really cared about you back then. I still do. You have always been important to me."

"I know." Kayo took the joint, looked at it, and pinched it out. "In some ways, Cary, we were never apart. We've been with each other all these years."

Cary slung his arm over Kayo's shoulder and rested his head on it. They sat like that for a moment. Suddenly, Cary sat up. "I almost forgot. I've been meaning to ask you this for months. Did you ever tell me Dan's last name? What was it?"

"Cavendish," Kayo answered.

THURSDAY, AUGUST 11, 2011

Columbiana City was at the end of a four-day heat wave. Cary was checking the thermometer on his front porch when *The 11 O'Clock News* began. It read eighty-nine degrees. He collapsed onto the wooden kitchen chair he had dragged onto the porch days earlier and tried to listen to the news. But the whirring noise of the fan set on the floor just inside the front door drowned out the television's audio. Cary, sapped by the heat, however, could not muster the strength or energy to get up and increase the set's volume. He had tried aiming the remote at the television by awkwardly reaching his arm around the front doorjamb, but the angle was too great; the signal was not reaching its target. He sat blankly staring into the dark, listening to the fan's hum. After ten minutes, he struggled to his feet and shuffled into his living room to adjust the television's volume.

Mac Hines greeted him. "Police forensic experts report no fingerprints or DNA was found on the items discovered two weeks ago in a garbage can near the Playas' parking lot," the anchor said. "The apparent lack of evidence, police report, warrants further examination of the crime scene and more tests."

A police spokesman appeared on the screen. "If we had DNA, we could at least determine the gender of Pete Gibson's murderer. We, therefore, acknowledge we could be searching for a man or a woman. We also realize the possibility that the woman last seen with Gibson was not a woman at all or possibly had not always been identified as a woman. As a result, we have to expand our search. We have to look outside the nine dots so to speak."

"Well," Mac said as he reappeared on-screen, "that certainly is an interesting development."

"It certainly is," Cary agreed as he stumbled back to the porch.

SUNDAY, AUGUST 14, 2011

Cary was making coffee in the kitchen at eight o'clock when KEHT's *Sunday A.M. News* began. He could hear Cassie Morales talking in the distance, but he could not decipher her words. He peeked around the corner into the living room. The lead story was a street fair. Cary toasted a bagel and grabbed a jar of strawberry jam from the cupboard. He peeked into the living room again. Cassie was reporting on an overnight accident involving a cab. The toasted bagel popped up. Then he heard it, the "Wedding March" by Mendelssohn. Odd, he thought. He peeked with curiosity around the corner one more time.

On the screen were two men in Speedo swim suits. They exuded the common stereotypes of gay men. The wispier, more effeminate one, was wearing a white swim suit and matching bowtie. The more masculine, more muscular, more hirsute man was in a black Speedo and bowtie. They were standing in a traditional church at the head of the aisle holding hands. A wedding party of several men dressed in a variety of leather S & M outfits lined alongside each man. A Catholic priest was standing in front of the couple. He grimaced with discomfort and disgust. A young boy, perhaps five years old, stood half way down the aisle holding a white satin pillow with two rings on it. He was wearing a white tuxedo with a pink bowtie. He was crying, fear in his face and posture. The man in the black Speedo let go of his partner's hand, turned toward the young boy, pulled a candy bar out of his Speedo, and offered it to the child. The "Wedding March" came to a screeching halt. An ominous deep voice said, "Is this what you want?" As the picture faded, "Vote Yes on 614. Save America's Marriages" appeared in bold red.

"Oh, my god," Cary gasped. "I have to call an immediate meeting."

He called Bren and asked her to contact Kayo and the others to inform them of the emergency meeting at The Pub at noon. Even with such short notice, everyone showed up with the exception of Stevon, who was working at Home Depot. Everyone else was there, including Abby Hoffman, the irate woman from the Shop-Wright parking lot. Cary was surprised and thankful.

"Welcome, Abby," he began. "It is great to have you on board. Now, did any of you see SAM's commercial this morning?" Cary asked. No one had. "I don't know how long it has been running, but I saw it just a few hours ago for the first time." He paused. "It is horrible. And it will cause problems. It will create a backlash against us. So, even though attacks against gays and their allies have been minimal for the past month, I think it is all about to change. The political temperature is about to rise. We are now officially in the campaign season. Therefore, I suggest we finalize our battle plan, determine what is payback and what is intended to scare and intimidate, and then pencil in a tentative schedule."

"OK," the team chimed in unison.

SATURDAY, AUGUST 20, 2011

It was several minutes into the broadcast when Cary tuned into The News @ 5. "According to the bartender," Cassie Morales was reporting, "he felt there would be a problem the minute the woman entered the room."

Cassie was standing in front of a small wine bar named Vini Vino known to cater to a wealthy, conservative clientele. A taped interview with the bartender appeared. A name plate pinned to the lapel of his black vest read "Stewart." "There were ten, maybe twelve customers," he explained. "She walked in looking like...well, she looked like Elizabeth Taylor in *Who's Afraid of Virginia Woolf?* You know, messy, disheveled, sort of cheap and overdone. Teased hair. Too much makeup. Tight clothes. She was like sixty years old and too heavy to wear tight clothes. Anyway, she came in and sat at the bar. That is when I noticed her jewelry. Gaudy, big, tacky. And she had this huge purse, maybe it was a bag, with bright, plastic baubles all over it. So she says to me, 'Do you like my jewels, honey?' Before I could form an answer, she says, 'I'll bet I'd like your jewels.' So, I just say, 'What can I get you?' and she says, 'Nothing special. Just the house white. While you pour that I need to use the restroom.' And that is when it happened."

"What happened, Stewart?" Cassie asked.

"She was gone a minute, maybe two, and then burst through the bathroom door flinging two or three tear gas canisters in back of her, as she bolted out the door."

"Was anyone hurt?"

"No, thank God. Everybody rushed out the door. I was gasping and gagging. Two of my customers did vomit outside, but I think they are fine now," Stewart answered. "And she was gone. Maybe a car was waiting for her. Who knows? Then, after we were able to clear the air and the police arrived, I went into the women's restroom to check and she had sprayed this sticky blood red substance all over everything in there. It's a mess!"

"Do you have any idea who she is, Stewart? Or what her purpose was?"

"Not a clue, Cassie."

Cassie noticed something over Stewart's shoulder as he spoke and stepped behind him to the closed wine bar door to examine it. Stewart turned as she walked around him. "Was this here before the incident?" she asked.

"No. We don't allow postings of any kind on our exterior. Frankly, I would think many of my regulars would disagree with that one."

The camera zoomed in on the door. A round decal, perhaps a bumper sticker, had been slapped on it. "No on I-614" it read.

TUESDAY, AUGUST 30, 2011

Teacher Killed in School Parking Lot silently screamed from the television as the ticker at the bottom of Kayo's screen crawled by. *The News @ 5* had just begun as he sat down on his worn 1970s sofa.

"We begin with the shocking news of a murder this afternoon in Norton Middle School's parking lot here in Columbiana City," Mac Hines stated with a hint of disbelief in his voice. "Kimberly Teller is on the scene. What can you tell us, Kimberly?"

The reporter appeared on the screen, yellow police tape marking off a section of the parking lot behind her. "A middle school teacher was gunned down just before lunch today by a fellow staff member," Kimberly said. "According to witnesses, a loud verbal exchange occurred between Lucia Corazon, the victim, and Brad Titus, the alleged gunman. Corazon had just announced at a staff meeting plans to start a Gay-Straight Alliance at the middle school. Teachers were in the building preparing for Thursday's first day of classes."

The camera pulled back to show two somber-faced women next to Kimberly. "I have two Norton teachers here, Nadine Harper and Kristina Volstead. "Nadine," Kimberly asked, "how did the staff respond to Ms. Corazon's plans for a GSA?"

"Very supportively." Most of the staff was totally behind Lucia's plan. Some did voice concerns that, while appropriate for high school students, a GSA might not be appropriate at a middle school. And a few had religious concerns. But, all in all, it was a civil and respectful discussion."

The other teacher, Kristina Volstead, interjected a comment. "Except for Brad. Mr. Titus became enraged that we were even having this discussion. 'Clubs like that shouldn't be allowed at any school,'" he said, 'especially one at which I work.' We should have had someone accompany Brad when we broke for lunch."

"Thank you, ladies," Kimberly said as the camera refocused on her. "That is when the shooting happened, when the staff broke for lunch. Witnesses say Titus followed Corazon to her car. A loud verbal exchange occurred and Titus is alleged to have pulled a small revolver out of his Norton hoodie and shot Corazon in the chest at close range. She died at the scene. Several staff members and a few students witnessed the shooting. Titus, who is a youth pastor at a nearby church, is now in police custody."

"Unbelievable," Mac said. "This tragedy could not have happened at a worse time. Will this incident impact the opening of school Thursday?" Mac asked.

"We don't know that. Back to you in the newsroom."

"Stay tuned to KEHT News for details regarding this shocking event and the opening of Norton Middle School," Mac advised, ending that report. Kayo stared in disbelief. *A teacher killing another teacher?* he thought. *That just doesn't happen. Unless, of course, you are in the middle of a war.*

WEDNESDAY, AUGUST 31, 2011

KEHT broke from its seven o'clock national news program *Sunrise USA* at 7:21. An urgent story was developing at Norton Middle School. Bren was watching on her laptop.

A short "Breaking News" alert interrupted the national program and Lacey Powers appeared on the screen. "We have a developing story at Norton Middle School where teacher Lucia Corazon was murdered yesterday. We go now to Kimberly Teller at the scene. What's going on there, Kimberly?" she asked.

Kimberly appeared in the school's parking lot, a flurry of people around her. "Within minutes of Spanish teacher Lucia Corazon's death yesterday, Norton students hit social media," Kimberly reported. "A memorial for the fallen educator was organized by mid-afternoon for 7:30 a.m., the time Ms. Corazon arrived like clockwork at school every morning. I have one of the organizers, Chloe, here. Chloe, why was Ms. Corazon here so early when school doesn't start until 8:30?"

The camera pulled back to include thirteen-year-old Chloe in the frame. "If she didn't have a meeting," the pale, tired-looking student said, "she was helping students with Spanish. Or listening to their problems. That's what she did. She was always there for us." Chloe's voice cracked. "I don't know why Coach Titus did this. Why couldn't he just have let her live her life? All she wanted to do was start a club, a support group for kids who needed it."

"Thanks, Chloe," Kimberly turned back to the camera. "Students have been arriving for this memorial for more than an hour, Lacey. There were maybe 200 at seven o'clock but the number is growing quickly." At this point, the camera panned further back and then rotated, showing the growing crowd. "I'm seeing a number of older teens, perhaps former students, here too. And adults. Parents. Staff members. There are a few rainbow flags in the crowd. A shrine of flowers, stuffed animals, balloons, and what appears to be Spanish or Mexican paraphernalia is growing quite rapidly where her car was usually parked."

"Do we know what is planned, Kimberly?"

"Principal David Springer told me it would be short. That is all I know."

"OK, Kimberly. We are going to break away for a moment," Lacey said, as she again appeared on the screen. "We've had a C-Met bus stall on the Riverside Park Bridge. This is causing quite a backup on 9th Avenue. KEHT is sending a crew to the scene. We'll return to Norton Middle School shortly. But first let's break for some commercial messages."

The immediate image was of two men standing at the end of a church aisle in Speedos. It was SAM's "Yes on 614" ad. "Well, that's a new definition of ironic," Bren gasped. A few other commercials followed. Then Lacey reappeared.

"We are going right to Norton Middle School and Kimberly Teller," she said with urgency.

"Yes, Lacey," the reporter whispered. "Principal Springer is about to speak." The camera swung from Kimberly to a man, fortyish, at a microphone.

"I wish we did not have to be here today," he began. "Oh, how I wish that." He swallowed. "But we are. We are here to honor Ms. Lucia Corazon." Principal Springer swallowed again. "I cannot explain what happened yesterday. We, the Norton community and the world as a whole, lost one wonderful teacher, friend, and human being." He paused. "Oh. Wow!" he said with surprise. "I just now realized how many of you are here. This crowd goes all the way to the main entrance. I don't think we are talking hundreds. Could this crowd be in the thousands?" He swallowed again. "What a wonderful tribute. Thank you all for coming. I am struggling to find something appropriate to say. I am wondering how we as a society, we as Americans, came to a point where we kill one another simply because we disagree. This can't go on. I hope and pray Lucia's death is not in vain. I hope and pray her unnecessary death is the last of its kind here in Columbiana City, here in the U.S., and in the world."

He paused and took a breath. "Now I want to introduce you to someone, someone few of you know or know about. And that says a lot about the state of affairs in Columbiana City and Columbiana today. She is here to lead us all in a moment of silence in honor of Ms. Corazon. Come on up, Denise." With that a Columbiana City police officer stepped from the front of the crowd and turned and faced it. "This is Denise Schmidt, Lucia's partner."

There was an audible gasp from the crowd, then whispered noises. Within seconds applause began. As the response rapidly grew louder and stronger, the camera pivoted to capture the crowd's thunderous reaction. When it peaked, the camera swung back to Officer Schmidt. She stood with her head bowed for a moment, and then, with tears streaming down her cheeks, looked up and motioned the crowd to quiet down, to be silent. Again, the camera rotated, capturing the solemn crowd. The silence lasted more than a minute. Then, from the back of the gathering, two deep male voices began chanting "Corazon! Corazon!" A few voices joined in at first, but a moment later, the entire crowd was chanting. The noise became a roar. The camera returned to the front of the chanting group. At the microphone, Principal Springer embraced Denise Schmidt, holding her sobbing head to his chest. They were not the only ones moved by the serious and somber tone of the moment. The TV camera zoomed in on students. Hugs and sobs were seen and heard throughout the crowd. The camera panned back to Kimberly.

"Back to you in the studio, Lacey," Kimberly whispered, her voice breaking with emotion. In the background, Principal Springer released Denise Schmidt, squeezed her hand, and bolted awkwardly toward the building's main door. The camera captured him pulling a white handkerchief from a pants pocket and dabbing his face before he entered.

In the back of the crowd, separated by at least twenty people, Cary and Kayo grieved. They were standing apart to avoid each other in public places, just like Cary had demanded at their final February Starbuck's meeting, just like they had done in the '70s. Tears flowing over their cheeks, Cary and Kayo smiled at each other across the crowd, proud of themselves. And their deep voices.

THURSDAY, SEPTEMBER 1, 2011

Columbiana City's Number One News Source--KEHT Channel 8--Thursday September 1, 2011--School Starts, Grieving Continues crawled across Cary's television as *The*

News @ 5 began. "School began today for Columbiana City schools, but things were not normal at Norton Middle School," Mac Hines opened. "Students and staff were still reeling from Tuesday's on-campus shooting of a beloved teacher. Kimberly Teller is at Norton with a report. Good evening, Kimberly."

"Good evening, Mac. Grief counselors attended Norton's first day of classes to assist students who might have trouble coping with the shocking situation, the murder just days ago of popular teacher Lucia Corazon," Kimberly reported.

Video of an interview with Principal David Springer taken earlier appeared. "How are things going, Mr. Springer?" Kimberly asked.

"As well as it can," he answered. "As a principal, this has been my biggest nightmare," he said. "You never want to deal with death at school. But when it happens on the first day of school, it makes it more of a challenge. We are prepared, however. We have capable professionals here today to help us all get through this. And we will."

Kimberly reappeared live. "A counselor told me they had been quite busy today and that several students were sent home because they were just too upset to stay at school. For a first day of school, Mac, the mood in this school's halls is very subdued. That's all from here."

"And in Oakville today," Mac began a new report as he reappeared on-camera, "a University of Columbiana fraternity faces suspension for videotaping members and young women having sex in its house and then posting them online."

FRIDAY, SEPTEMBER 2, 2011

GSA Meets at Norton was the first thing Cary saw when the picture appeared on his television. It was crawling under the *NoonNews8* logo on the screen. Mac Hines' image followed. "We are immediately going to Kimberly Teller at Norton Middle School," he said with urgency. "Good afternoon, Kimberly."

"Hi, Mac," Kimberly said softly. "I'm standing outside Lucia Corazon's classroom. Norton's Gay-Straight Alliance is meeting today for the first time behind that door." She turned and motioned toward the door. "While Ms. Corazon is not here to follow through with her proposal to start the group, students went ahead with the idea, organized the meeting, and honored their teacher. I counted at least forty students going into that room when the meeting began. Just a few minutes ago, I heard a loud cheer and a young man stepped out the door and posted this on it." Kimberly stepped aside and the camera swung over her shoulder to display a sign. "Corazon Club" it said. Each "o" was in the shape of a pink heart. "Back to you, Mac."

"Thanks, Kimberly. And in Stover today, a cab driver was charged with DWI while on duty."

SATURDAY, SEPTEMBER 3, 2011

"It's funny, isn't it, how we both showed up here at the same time and for the same reason?" Kayo asked Cary as they sat next to each other on the patch of grass at The Pub.

"Yeah. Apparently, brilliant minds really *do* think alike."

"Grieving minds, actually."

Cary put his arm around Kayo's shoulders. "I'm having a real difficult time processing the death of that teacher," he said. "She shouldn't have died."

"I know."

The duo sat in silence, Cary with his head lowered, Kayo facing forward with his eyes closed. Minutes passed. Cary spoke first.

"I'm feeling guilt, man. More guilt."

"Why?" Kayo asked.

"I'm wondering if what we've been doing the past few months, our raisin' hell, could have contributed to that tight ass Titus killing her. You know, it could have pissed him off so much it pushed him over the edge." Cary dug his left heel in the grass, making a divot. "She shouldn't have died in this war. She was just a teacher who wanted to start a Gay-Straight Alliance."

"I know, man. "I've been thinking about that, too," Kayo said, opening his eyes. "I'm feeling the same guilt." A single tear, almost heart shaped, rolled down his cheek, fell onto his tie-dye T-shirt, and shattered. Kayo rested his head on Cary's shoulder.

MONDAY, SEPTEMBER 5, 2011

Because it was a holiday, Labor Day, *The News @ 5* did not begin until 6:00. A major golf tournament held in Columbiana for the first time in twenty-five years took precedence. But it was not until after the six thirty break, that Save America's Marriages' Labor Day picnic was covered. And then, only briefly.

"The organization leading the drive to repeal gay marriage, Save America's Marriages, held a picnic today at Flaming Waters State Park south of Stover," Marletta Gaines read, as film of the picnic was shown. The TV camera showed people eating, children playing, and American flags flying. Then, it panned to Al Kirk, wearing black slacks and wingtips, a long sleeve white shirt and an American flag-patterned tie, at a microphone addressing the picnickers. "We do not, under any circumstances, condone what happened this past week at Norton Middle School," he said, making the campaign's first public comments on Lucia Corazon's murder, "but we are praying for our friend Brad Titus, who is a valiant Christian, if not perhaps a misguided crusader for Christian values. We believe, however, that woman died, not because Brad is a Christian, but because she was not." Video coverage of the event ended.

Marletta returned to the screen. "Our cameraman, J.C. Ogden, who was at the picnic for several hours, reports that none of SAM's speakers acknowledged what day it is, the purpose of the holiday, our labor force, or the achievements of the labor movement. So I will. Today is Labor Day. Just a reminder." Marletta then smiled with satisfaction. The screen blacked out for a moment and a commercial for a Labor Day car sale at Nick Carney Motors appeared.

Nick Carney Motors? a surprised and confused Cary thought. *Carney was Lisa's maiden name. Nick is our son's name. I didn't know we had a Nick Carney Motors in the area. That is really weird.*

SUNDAY, SEPTEMBER 11, 2011

There was no crawling ticker when *Sunday AM News* began at 7:00. There was no self-promoting of KEHT visible. There was no familiar logo. All that was seen was an empty anchor desk. All that was heard was somber music.

Cassie Morales, dressed in a black skirt suit with white blouse, entered the set from stage right and sat at the desk. "Today is September 11, 2011. It is the tenth anniversary of one of America's darkest days," she said. "We will delay the local news and go directly to our affiliate in New York City and the site of the 9-11 Memorial and follow what is happening there."

Other than the voices reading the names of the more than 3,000 people killed that day, there was no sound. A camera panned across the memorial and through the crowd of onlookers, frequently stopping at a face that poignantly captured the emotions of the moment. An occasional American flag was shown. After ten minutes, Cassie Morales quietly said, "We'll be right back."

The screen went blank for a moment. Then, the familiar image of a one-hundred-plus-story tower collapsing appeared. Shrieks were heard. Suddenly, the action and sound froze. The tower stopped falling. The shrieks went silent. A resonant male voice spoke. "Religious extremists did this," it said. The picture quickly changed, showing two middle-age men, dressed in suits with white boutonnieres in their lapels standing in front of a minister in a crowded church. They were smiling. Just as the minister opened his mouth to begin the ceremony, an oversized open hand came from screen right and slapped both men, knocking them to the ground. Bruised and bloodied, they looked at the camera, confusion and pain in their eyes. The resonant voice returned. "Don't let religious extremists do this," it said. Superimposed over this image "Vote NO on 614" emerged, as the men resiliently stood, ignoring their pain, and faced the minister.

"Wow," gasped Cary "Powerful."

He saw the commercial three more times that day. It ran hourly on all Columbiana television stations.

MONDAY, SEPTEMBER 12, 2011

Cary had stopped at Starbuck's on the way to his office and picked up an abandoned *Columbiana City Chronicle* from a neighboring table to peruse while he sipped his coffee. *KEHT Releases Gaines* stared back at him from the front of the local news section. Surprised, he read the article. Marletta Gaines, according to the report, had apparently piqued the ire of Save America's Marriage, its supporters, and conservatives in general by reporting what cameraman J.C. Ogden had told her regarding the SAM Labor Day Picnic. They flooded the station with angry phone calls, emails, and texts saying Ogden's comment simply was not true; the holiday had been acknowledged by the first speaker, apparently prior to Ogden's arrival. They were appalled Gaines believed him and then repeated the comment on the air without verifying the information. As a result, they demanded Gaines be fired. A spokesman for KEHT said they had no other choice.

That is just a bit hypocritical, Cary thought. *TV news reporters are relying more and more on nonprofessional eyewitnesses and social media to support them. Some of the complainers themselves,* Cary thought, *could have misreported stories in the past through social media posts picked up by professional news teams.* Cary also found it surprising how easily management caved in to the right-wing remands. *There must be more to this than is being reported,* Cary theorized. *Or maybe there's more about Marletta Gaines than we know.*

Cary turned the page. *Accused Teacher Killer Hires Lawyer* was the first thing Cary saw.

THURSDAY, SEPTEMBER 15, 2011

Veteran Lawyer Gunned Down read the creeping headline at the beginning of *The News @ 5.* "We begin the news with the mysterious murder of a local lawyer, Digby Owen Arrabel," announced Lacey Powers. "D.O. Arrabel, as he was known professionally, was gunned down as he arrived at his office around 7:30 this morning. His body was found next to his car in the alley in back of his office. He was found by a jogger. There appear to be no witnesses. Arrabel was recently hired by accused teacher killer Brad Titus.

"Arrabel began his career in the 1970s as a court-appointed lawyer for a number of arrested anti-Vietnam War activists. Some complained at the time he failed to defend them properly and that he was responsible for their being found guilty or for their unexpectedly long terms. He, however, was never investigated by the American Bar Association or charged. In 1984, Arrabel ran unsuccessfully for the state legislature as a conservative Republican. D.O.

Arrabel was sixty-eight years old. He leaves a wife, Clara, two children, and four grandchildren."

Cary hardly paid attention to Lacey's report. He already knew all about it.

SATURDAY, SEPTEMBER 17, 2011

Cary was watching college football, the University of Columbiana Coyotes against Grayson State's Grizzlies, a lopsided matchup with the favored Coyotes holding a 39-3 halftime lead. He rose to go to the bathroom when the commercial appeared.

A beautiful bride in an elegant white gown and veil and a handsome tuxedoed groom face the camera. They don't look happy. Solemn church organ music plays in the background. "I don't," they say in unison. The camera zeroes in on the bride's parents in the front row. "I don't," they say in sync. The camera moves to an elderly couple back a row. "I don't," they say as one. The camera zooms across the aisle to the groom's side and focuses on an attractive middle-age African American couple who say "I don't" together. The camera moves next to them. Identical college-age twin girls stare at the camera just long enough for "Cindy and Mindy Forsythe, daughters of Republican U.S. Sen. Stuart Forsythe" to appear superimposed across their torsos. "I don't," they say in unison. The camera moves back a row. "I don't," say two men together. They are holding hands. The camera floats between them and back a row. U of C Coyote quarterback and Heisman Trophy candidate Aaron Lanphere and his girlfriend, cheerleader Matisse Dillard, say "I don't" as one. The camera swoops to the church's back row and focuses on two women. They are thirty-year-old Academy Award-winning actress and Columbiana City favorite daughter Taryn Masters and her long-rumored partner tennis pro Allison Fritz. "I don't support Initiative 614. Vote No!" they proudly say together. The screen darkens and a bold red "Vote NO on 614!" appears.

Cary stared in shock. *What an incredible ad. That was the first time Taryn and Allison have publicly acknowledged their relationship,* he thought. *It took this campaign to do it. That is fuckin' far out!*

SUNDAY, SEPTEMBER 19, 2011

Columbiana City's Number One News Source--KEHT Channel 8--September 19, 2011--Student Pray-In Surprises SAM, NOD inched across Cary's television. It was six o'clock and the news had just begun. Cassie Morales sat at the news desk.

"A surprise pray-in to defeat Initiative 614 organized online by and for teenagers drew more than 800 participants this morning. It was held in the Norton Middle School parking lot where a memorial for slain teacher Lucia Corazon was held recently," Cassie announced. "Organizers had hoped to attract exactly 614 youths, but were surprised and excited by the large turnout." Footage from the parking lot pray-in appeared. Norton Middle School loomed in the background. A young woman with shocking pink hair appeared on the screen.

"We decided to do this," she told an invisible interviewer, "to tell the state's voters that we, the next generation, are opposed to Initiative 614. The right to marry should include anyone who loves another person enough to want to marry them. Love is love."

An off-camera voice asked if this group had a name.

"Yes," the girl said. "We are the Children of God and we promote the true Christian principles of tolerance, inclusion, and love for everyone. Our intent is to erase the hypocrisies of many of our Christian predecessors."

"What is your name?" the unseen reporter asked.

"Paloma," the girl answered.

Cassie, sitting at the anchor desk, returned to the screen. "We contacted No on Discrimination to see if they were aware of the pray-in. A spokesperson said they were not and were appreciative of the overwhelming support."

"We also spoke with Save America's Marriages cochairman Sandi Iglesias this afternoon. She told us she doubted NOD's claim that they were not involved. This, Iglesias added, was just another attempt by the gay agenda to seduce our children. She then questioned why this religious event was held on school property. 'When conservative Christians wish to hold a religious function on school property,' she explained, 'we are always rudely reminded of the alleged separation of church and state.'"

"Oh, my god, woman," Cary exhaled in disbelief. "You are such a bitch. I would hate to be married to you."

SATURDAY, OCTOBER 8, 2011

As Kayo stepped out his apartment door and into the building's stale-smelling hall, he nearly tripped over a white paper bag blocking his path. He picked it up, looked inside, and chuckled, filling the claustrophobic hall with his signature laugh.

He brought the bag to his kitchen, laid its contents, two jewel bedecked bagels, on a plate and thought, *I'll eat these when I get home.* Then he read the note accompanying the unexpected birthday gift and smiled. "Do you like my jewels?" wrote Jules.

Kayo then left to get his birthday present to himself, a haircut.

SUNDAY, OCTOBER 9, 2011

The teaser had been running across the bottom of KEHT's newscasts for two weeks. *Town Hall Meeting--Initiative 614-Gay Marriage--Sun Oct 9 @ 4* it read. Cary knew he was going to watch it. He also knew he was going to get pissed off as all hell.

This is going to be a train wreck, he thought. *A disorganized debate. Charges and countercharges. False statements unchallenged. Embarrassing statements made by both sides. Embarrassing people representing both sides. Controversy. Conflict. Anger. Hate. Entertaining television.* KEHT said the special program was being aired to educate Columbiana's electorate. That may have been partially true. But Cary knew the real reason. KEHT had to fulfill the Federal Communications Commission's requirement that all stations offer free public service broadcasting. *What percentage of the viewing public, and voting public, would be watching a debate at four o'clock on Sunday afternoon during football season?* Cary thought.

The graphic was bold: *Town Hall Meeting: A Debate on I-614.* The music was full of tension. The graphic and music faded. Mac Hines appeared, standing in front of a studio audience and holding a microphone. "Good afternoon. I'm Mac Hines," he introduced himself. "No issue on next month's ballot is more divisive or controversial than Initiative 614. It seeks to repeal state legislation legalizing gay marriage in Columbiana. Voting yes will repeal the law and bar gay marriage; voting no will allow the law approved in February to take effect.

Representatives of both sides are here." Mac motioned to a long table facing the audience. "For Save America's Marriages, the sponsor of the initiative, we have Rev. Al Kirk, Sandi Iglesias, and Fr. Padrig O'Casey. Representing No on Discrimination are Davis Wells, sociologist Dr. Gwen Potts, and University of Columbiana student body president Russell Kim. Our studio audience consists of supporters of both sides. We ask our audience members to be polite and respectful of all speakers whether you agree with them or not. If you have a question for our panelists, raise your hand and I'll try to get to you as quickly as I can with the microphone." Hands immediately went up throughout the studio. Mac stepped closer to an elderly woman sitting on the aisle nearby. "Hello. You get the first question," Mac said with a smile as he tilted the microphone toward her.

"My question is for either Mr. Kirk or Ms. Iglesias," she said.

"*Reverend* Kirk," Mac corrected the woman.

She ignored him. "Why is stopping gay men and lesbian women from marrying so important to you?"

Cary sat and listened to the answer. Nothing was said that surprised him. He listened to all the other questions and comments. For the most part, nothing unexpected or unscripted was said by either side. They all were biased and full of half-truths, assumptions, and skewed statistics.

Only two moments stood out for Cary. They were the only moments worth remembering and for very different reasons. The first came when a male audience member supporting the initiative attacked Dr. Potts for being a Socialist.

"I'm not a Socialist," she responded.

"Mr. Hines said you are," countered the man angrily.

"I said she is a sociologist, sir," Mac corrected with a slight laugh.

"What's that?" the man asked.

The other memorable moment was a personal one. It occurred rather late in the hour-long program. Mac reached the microphone to a man sitting in the far end seat of the back row. Until that second, the camera had never shown him.

"Oh, my god!" Cary gasped. "It's Kayo. Only...oh, my god!" Kayo's graying ponytail was gone. His short-cropped hair had been dyed a shade darker than its original color, but with gray streaks. He was wearing a charcoal colored suit, white dress shirt and striped tie. He looked like Al Kirk. Kayo took the microphone.

"My question is for Mr. Kirk," Kayo said, emphasizing the incorrect title. "Your name is Alexander Kirk. Right? Do you know what my name is?"

"No. Should I?"

"My name is Kirk Alexander." Hushed laughter and whispered comments filled the studio. "Our names are alike. Only they are not. They are opposites. We probably are alike in many other ways. And in many ways, we are opposites. But if either of us were shot in the heart, we would both feel the same pain, die the same death. Mr. Kirk, your initiative is shooting me in the heart." Kayo handed the microphone back to Mac. There was a beat of silence and then simultaneously the opponents of the measure in the audience began to cheer. It was difficult to hear him over the noise, but Mac Hines said, "Point well made, Mr. Alexander."

Cary remembered nothing else about the Town Hall Meeting. Except that he was very proud of Kayo.

MONDAY, OCTOBER 10, 2011

Surprising Arrest at Conover Park was the cryptic headline crawling across Cary's television screen, as he watched KEHT's *Morning News*. He was eating a bowl of Frosted Flakes, and feeling a bit like Tony the Tiger. The elation he had felt watching Kayo on *Town Hall Meeting* the day before had stayed with him through the night and he was still feeling "G-r-r-r-e-a-t!" He put down the bowl, picked up his coffee cup, and sipped.

"An unexpected arrest was made yesterday afternoon in Conover Park," Lacey Powers read, "when Columbiana City police interrupted a thirty-five-year-old man performing a sex act on a fifteen-year-old boy in a secluded section of the park. Police had received several tips that a group of teenage boys was planning to assault gay men, a police spokesman said. The tips, the representative said, were the result of careless use of social media. The arrested man was identified as Carlos Iglesias, husband of Save America's Marriages cochairman

Sandi Iglesias. The arrest took place while Ms. Iglesias participated on KEHT's Town Hall Meeting yesterday. The boy was released to his parents.

"While Conover Park has been rumored for decades to be a clandestine meeting place for gay men, activity there had dropped off in recent years, according to the spokesman. The internet and social media appear to be responsible for that change," she added.

"What the hell?" Cary laughed. "That is just plain funny. Embarrassing for him. Tragic for the boy. But fucking funny. The timing couldn't be more perfect."

TUESDAY, OCTOBER 11, 2011

614 Race Tightens, Poll Shows glided across the screen. Cary didn't notice. He was already asleep in his recliner. He'd come home from school around nine thirty, looked at his mail, checked phone messages and email, and plopped onto the gray Lazy-Boy just minutes before *The 11 O'Clock News* began. But he was asleep before its theme music started.

"With less than a month to go before Election Day, support for Initiative 614 seems to be slipping," Mac Hines told no one at the Foreman home. "The race for gay marriage is getting closer. The number approving preventing gays and lesbians from marrying has slipped to 50 percent while those against the proposal is at 44 percent. Undecided voters make up 6 percent. The McGraw-Pitts Research poll was taken October 6. One thousand registered Columbiana voters were surveyed. There is a rate of error of 4 percent."

Cary squirmed in his chair, made a throat-clearing noise, and wriggled a smile as if pleased by something.

FRIDAY, OCTOBER 14, 2011

It was just after eleven in the morning when Cary sat down in Starbuck's. His steaming coffee rested in front of him, a copy of *The Columbiana City Chronicle* next to it. Cary had purposely left home earlier than normal so he could leisurely read the newspaper before going to school. He sipped his drink as he scanned the front page headlines and then folded over the first section to see what the lead story was on the local news section.

Race at Core of Firing, Gaines Claims stretched across the top of the section's front page. Cary began reading the article. "Marletta Gaines revealed yesterday why she was fired from KEHT last month. Race, she said, was the reason."

Interesting, thought Cary. *So it wasn't because she reported incorrect information given to her by a station cameraman.* He scanned the article, looking for highlights.

"Thirty-one-year-old Gaines…studied broadcast journalism…met her husband at the University of Columbiana…husband majored in government and went on to law school…became a lawyer for the American Civil Liberties Union."

Who cares? Cary thought. *That's not newsworthy and it has nothing to do with race.* When he read, however, that Gaines' husband Simon Wright is the son of Shop-Wright founder and political conservative Zebulon Wright, Cary sat up, his curiosity aroused. He pulled the newspaper closer and tilted his upper body over it. His posture reflected his focus on and interest in what he was reading. His body language indicated he did not want to be interrupted.

"Hey, dude."

Cary looked up, a bit annoyed. Stevon stood across the table, smiling at him over a foam-topped cup. "Hi," Cary said with irritation, "but I don't think I qualify as 'dude.' I'm too old for that. That's *your* generation. My generation said '*man.*'"

Stevon snickered and said, "I know," waited a beat and added, "man." He smiled devilishly. "Was that better?"

Cary released a short laugh. His posture relaxed. "Hey, sit. Join me. I was just reading this Marletta Gaines interview."

"I was going to read it, too. Just as soon as I logged on," Stevon said as he sat and pulled his laptop from his backpack.

"The article says Gaines' husband is Simon Wright, son of Zebulon Wright. Did you know that?" Cary asked.

"Yep."

"And Zebulon was opposed to his son's involvement with Gaines from the beginning of their relationship."

"I figured as much. Old Man Wright practically bankrolls the right wing here, Stevon explained unnecessarily.

"Yeah," Cary agreed. "But he tried to conceal his true feelings with a façade of civility, according to the interview. But it was an icy civility, Gaines says."

"OK. I'm on," Stevon interrupted. "And I have the interview in front of me. So where are you?"

"Bottom of the first page, where Simon joins the ACLU as a lawyer."

Stevon scrolled for a moment. "OK. I see. And Simon's dad goes on a rant. Gaines says Zebulon screamed at her, blaming her for seducing his son into a life of interracial sin and converting him to liberal politics." Stevon snorted with disgust. "Oh, brother."

"According to Gaines, because Zebulon had raised Simon at an arm's distance, he had had no idea what Simon's political views were or that they had been developing since his adolescence, long before he met Gaines." Cary stopped. "This could be on Jerry Springer or Maury Povich," he said with a laugh.

"Oh my god, Cary. Are you reading this? The shit really hit the fan when Simon announced his engagement to Gaines weeks after being hired by the ACLU. Old Zeb called a rushed meeting with his son and with close personal friend and minister, Rev. Al Kirk. Can you believe that?"

"Sure I can. Of course, Simon, being a lawyer and suspicious of what might happen, carried a backpack to the meeting; a recorder inside the bag taped the entire proceedings."

Stevon looked up. "Can you imagine sitting in on that meeting?"

"Well, it says right here what happened," Cary answers. "Zebulon threatened Simon at one point. He said, 'If you marry that filthy negress, I will disown you, disinherit you. You will be on your own.'"

"And," Stevon added, "Kirk is heard in the background saying, 'Don't call the bitch a negress. It's too respectful.'" That was followed by a chorus of cackling.

"Here is the coffin nail, Stevon. Zebulon then added, 'I will do whatever I have to do to bring you and that black bitch down.'" *Now that is interesting,* Cary thought. *That is newsworthy.*

"So, Marletta Gaines got fired," Stevon said as he looked at Cary, "because of a powerful man's vendetta and bigoted political views, not her on-air conduct or comment."

"The elder Wright and Kirk had simply been waiting for an opportune time to act, she theorizes," Cary read aloud. "Gaines' moment of, perhaps, poor judgment as a reporter offered them their opportunity."

"And then they hastily organized a phone-in and write-in campaign to get Gaines fired." Stevon looked at his coffee cup. "Damn. I forgot all about this. It's probably cold." He spooned the frothy topping off the cup and took his first sip. "Nope. It's still OK," he mumbled as he put the cup down and gazed out the window. His mocha-toned skin blanched as centuries of pain burned his eyes. "But this whole interview isn't OK."

"It gets worse, Stevon. Gaines says here an unnamed source at the station told her Zebulon Wright even threatened to pull all Shop-Wright advertising from KEHT as well as sponsorship of the annual Winter Lights Festival. Station management caved."

"Shit."

Cary looked at Stevon and touched his hand. The gentle pat brought Stevon's attention back to Cary and the interview. He looked at Cary for a moment and then bowed his head, staring unfocussed through the pain at the table. "Those racist bastards," Cary charged through gritted teeth. "Their bigotry isn't limited to gays, lesbians, bisexuals, and transgender people. It still includes African Americans. In the twenty-first century. Why am I not surprised?"

SUNDAY, OCTOBER 16, 2011

Cary heard the shrill, staccato music from the kitchen. He was at the dinette table attempting the Sudoku from the *Sunday Columbiana City Chronicle*. Then he heard the deep voice repeatedly saying "Breaking News." He jumped up and tore into the living room and looked at his television.

Gunshots at NOD Cruise raced over and over across the screen, faster than usual, indicating urgency. A glaring "Breaking News" graphic filled the monitor above the running headline. Cary looked at his watch. "4:17" stared back. *The Sunday News,* he thought, *doesn't usually come on until five.* Cassie Morales appeared, standing in front of the anchor desk. She appeared to be listening to her earpiece. Her hair was not perfectly combed. She looked up at the camera.

"We are getting a report of gunshots, at least two, as the Queen of the Lake was preparing to dock at the pier on Lake Conover," Cassie said slowly, somewhat uncertainly. She paused, as if listening. "The paddle-wheeler had been rented for the afternoon by No on Discrimination for a fundraiser. We are told 614 tickets had been sold for the event." She paused again. "Oh, yes. This is the event that brought comedienne and actress Helen DeWitt to town. She and her partner pop singer Katie Quinn entertained the crowd while the boat cruised the lake." Cassie appeared to be listening again. "OK," she said. "That is all we know now. We hope to have more information on *The News @ 5.*" The camera lingered on Cassie who looked with confusion off-set to the left. Programming then returned to the interrupted final round of a golf tournament Cary had not been watching.

Cary returned to the kitchen and his Sudoku.

When *The News @ 5* began, *Breaking News* were the first words on the creeping ticker. They were followed by *No Deaths at NOD Shooting.* Cassie Morales appeared, seated at the news desk. She was composed and better coiffed than she had been during her emergency broadcast.

"As reported earlier," Cassie said, "a shooting occurred this afternoon at a No on Discrimination fundraiser on Lake Conover. Witnesses reported hearing at least two gunshots as the paddle wheeler Queen of the Lake neared the pier. Entertainers Helen DeWitt and Katie Quinn and 614 people were on board." Cassie turned to a different camera. "Kimberly Teller is at the pier. Good evening, Kimberly. What can you tell us?"

"Good evening, Cassie." The reporter stood on the pier, numerous people roaming about behind her, some visibly shaken. "The good news is no one was hurt. But, according to Taylor Mathis here," and the camera zoomed out to include a woman in her twenties in the picture, "it could have been worse. What do you mean by that, Taylor?"

"As we were nearing the dock, Helen and Davis Wells were making some final comments and thanking everyone, when suddenly there were two rapid-fire blasts and the mirror in back of Helen shattered, spraying glass everywhere. I saw Helen and Davis fall forward and crouch down to avoid the glass. At first, I couldn't tell if they'd been hit or had jumped out of the way. Then I saw them get up and scramble away and I could see they were OK. As far as I know, no one was hurt. Somebody retrieved one of the bullets and one of the security people said it was from a rifle."

"Thank you, Taylor. That is all we know at this time, Cassie, so I will throw it back to you in the newsroom," Kimberly said.

Cassie didn't respond right away. She seemed to be listening to her earpiece. "OK," she said with surprise. "We have more breaking news related to this story. Apparently, a person of interest has been taken into custody."

MONDAY, OCTOBER 17, 2011

NOD Shooter Caught by Unexpected Hero inched across Cary's television screen as the morning news began. Lacey Powers smiled and greeted her early rising viewers. "Details of yesterday's shooting at Conover Lake and the capture of the gunman reveal unusual courage by the surprising and, perhaps, ironic hero," Lacey announced. "Cassie Morales is at Lake Conover. Good morning, Cassie."

The reporter stood in an empty parking lot. Shrubs and trees formed a woodsy backdrop. The gray autumn dawn's light matched the concrete surrounding her. Cassie, standing out in a lemon yellow jacket with the KEHT logo over her heart, greeted the anchor. "Good morning, Lacey. Plainclothes officers had been assigned to security patrol on the lakeshore because of the potential for violence at a No on Discrimination fundraiser.

"An officer spotted a suspicious man here in the parking lot," and Cassie made a sweeping motion with her arm, "prior to the cruise's departure." Stock footage of the Queen of the Lake setting sail appeared on the screen. Cassie continued her report, voicing over the film. "The man had been hovering in the background, neither interacting with any of the passengers as they waited on shore nor making an effort to board the boat later. When the ship departed, he returned to his car."

Cassie reappeared on screen, walking toward the shrubs and trees lining the shoreline. "The officer left the area when the paddle wheeler departed, patrolling the woods for anything unusual. When she saw the Queen of the Lake returning nearly two hours later, the officer began walking back to the parking lot. Spotting an opening in the overgrowth near the lot, the officer stepped into the woods to find a vantage point from where both the suspicious man and the Queen of the Lake could be observed." Cassie inched her way through the thick greenery as she spoke. She struggled with several branches blocking her path. Others jabbed at her. "The officer found a vantage point above the shoreline," Cassie continued, "and crouched in wait." Cassie crouched.

"Within minutes, according to the police report, the officer observed the man exiting his car, opening the trunk, taking out a long package, and walking toward the shore," Cassie went on. "He disappeared into the overgrowth and, the officer noted, crouched and unwrapped the package. Tree trunks and clusters of leaves blocked the officer's vision, making it difficult to identify the package's contents. But the officer suspected it was a rifle." The camera swung behind Cassie and shot over her shoulder, exposing what the officer might have seen. "Anticipating the man's actions, the officer's weapon was readied and drawn.

"As the Queen of the Lake neared the pier, the man suddenly stood, rapidly aimed a rifle at the boat, and shot. The officer fired almost simultaneously, hitting the man in the right shoulder. The startled man fell to the ground in pain, inadvertently pitching the rifle forward, out of his reach. The officer immediately retrieved the weapon and called for support and an aid unit."

A still photo of a female police officer appeared on the screen. "The officer has been identified as six-year veteran Denise Schmidt," Lacey said, her face hinting a proud smile.

"Oh, my god," gasped Cary. "That's that Corazon teacher's partner!"

TUESDAY, OCTOBER 18, 2011

Marine ID'd as NOD Shooter read the short crawling headline. Lacey Powers read the details to begin the *Morning News*. "The suspect in yesterday's shooting at a No on Discrimination fundraiser at Lake Conover has been identified as former Marine Kirk N. Dahl of Poipu Beach, Kauai."

"What?" Cary gasped even louder than he had when the police officer who captured Dahl had been named. *Poipu Beach? No one is from Poipu Beach. People go to Poipu Beach. To vacation. To relax. To escape. To hide,* he thought. *And why does the name Kirk N. Dahl sound familiar?*

SUNDAY, OCTOBER 23, 2011

Chronicle Opposes I-614 announced the headline of the *Sunday Columbiana City Chronicle* editorial column. This was a bit of a surprise because the *Chronicle* had been traditionally a conservative newspaper siding politically with the views of the state's powerful, wealthy, old-fashioned, and cautious business and financial community.

"Wow!" Cary whispered to himself. "That is unexpected."

While the newspaper's editorial board had been publishing its endorsements for elective offices and the other ballot initiatives during the past month, it had purposely waited until the last moment to reveal its stand on the election's most controversial and contentious campaign. By making this announcement only a week before Election Day, it hoped to eliminate its becoming a catalyst for more violence. Its endorsement, in fact, referred to the numerous incidents of violence and criminal activity that had been plaguing the state since the passage of the gay marriage act in February. "While it has been difficult to link either Save America's Marriages or No on Discrimination to any of the acts or to separate the shameful and embarrassing incidents from the core issue," the editorial stated, "we believe we could not allow the spate of violent, hateful behavior from people on both sides of the issue to impact our endorsement."

In making its decision, the board cited changing times, a repudiation of any form of government-approved discrimination, separation of church and state, the unfairness of public votes pitting a majority group against a minority, and simple decency as the deciding factors. The editorial ended with a powerful statement: "We resoundingly say 'Vote No on Initiative 614.' It is time. It is fair. It is the right thing to do."

Cary stared at the editorial in disbelief. *Never,* he thought, *did I expect to see a Columbiana state legislature and governor approve any form of gay rights, let alone gay marriage. Never did I expect to see the conservative, traditional* Chronicle *make such a progressive statement. And never did I expect to see my gay, lesbian, bisexual, and transgender friends actually have a chance to win an election by popular vote in this state.* Cary paused a moment and let out a little laugh. *Maybe I've been looking at the world through my 1970s-tinted glasses too long.*

TUESDAY, NOVEMBER 1, 2011

It was Election Day in Columbiana. *Follow Election Results Tonight on KEHT- -Beginning @ 8 on 8* flowed cross the bottom of every KEHT program all day. The constant promotion was necessary to win the ratings war. All other Columbiana TV stations would be covering election results, too, and thus, they also would be over-hyping their coverage. Watching election coverage was an honored Columbiana tradition because the results were almost always known by midnight. Unlike other states in which mail-in voting had been recently allowed and encouraged and, as a result, final outcomes often delayed for days, even weeks, the State of Columbiana had continued requiring voters to go to their neighborhood polls to vote. Tallies, under this time-tested system were done immediately upon closing at 8:00 and forwarded to each county's election headquarters. Results, complete results, official results could be known in hours.

Not everyone, though, was physically able to vote in person. To qualify as an absentee voter in Columbiana was quite challenging: one would have to be in the military, working or studying outside the state, physically unable to get to the polls, or residing in a foreign country. To prove these last two, one would have to jump through more hoops than a Cirque du Soleil acrobat.

Whether to allow mail-in voting or not had been on the ballot three times during the past decade. Traditional Columbianans had stayed the course when it came to absentee voting. It was soundly defeated each time. Today the traditional State of Columbiana was voting on changing the terms of an even more contentious issue, marriage.

Cary called Kayo at eleven in the morning.

"Hello," Kayo answered.

"It's me."

"I know. They've invented caller ID. Why are you calling? I thought we avoided the phone. Flying under the radar. Not being seen in public together. All that activist-radical-spy-versus-spy shit."

"True, "Cary agreed, "but I was thinking we should go to the NOD victory party tonight."

"Why? Do you think we're gonna win?"

"Something in my gut. A feeling. I cancelled my evening class. Told my students we'd make it up later in the term. I planned to watch the results at home. But now I think we should go."

"Why?" Kayo pressed.

"I think history is going to be made tonight. I think we need to be part of it. Man, we deserve it. You more than me. Come on, Kayo. Let's be seen together in public again."

"OK. But I'll have to meet you there. I'm having dinner at six with a neighbor. A young guy, maybe forty. He saw me on *Town Hall Meeting*. He wants to buy me dinner as a thank you."

"I'll bet that's not all he wants," Cary snarked.

"What? Oh," Kayo said with a tinge of confusion in his voice. "Oh!" The tinge faded. "Shut up! The victory party is still scheduled for the Abernathy Mansion, right?"

"Yeah, man. Be there. Eight thirty."

Cary arrived at the Abernathy Mansion at 8:20 and stared at its dignified, ivy-covered brick façade for a moment. He watched a large "No on Discrimination" banner undulate in the breeze across the front of the mansion and then he climbed the marble stairs and stepped in the stately doorway. He fought his way through the crowded foyer and into a large room to see if any results had been posted. He found two giant screen televisions at the front of the room, perhaps used as a ballroom decades earlier. The televisions were airing KEHT. A ticker showed some early results from local races, but nothing statewide yet. Then, just as Cary thought he should head closer to the entrance to find Kayo when he arrived, the ticker showed its first results for initiatives. *Initiative 614 Yes: 4,386, No: 4,752.* Cary did a double take. A roar erupted around him. *What?* he thought. *We're ahead?*

But Cary did not have time to process the surprise. He turned and wound his way through the crowd to the entrance where he hoped to find Kayo. Kayo arrived a few minutes later, running up the stairs.

"First results show us ahead," Cary yelled, as Kayo approached. "Can you believe that?"

"Yes, I can. But why are you surprised? I thought you said you had a gut feeling about tonight."

"Oh, that was bullshit, man. To get you here," Cary admitted. "Hey, how did your dinner go?"

"He just wanted to thank me."

"Oh."

"Don't sound so disappointed, man," Kayo said. "He wants to thank me again tomorrow night."

"All right!" Cary shouted. But the crowd's excited noise muffled his hopeful reaction.

The duo weaved their way through the throng of NOD supporters until they could clearly see a television screen. New figures showed the "no" vote maintaining its lead. *Initiative 614 Yes: 6,891, No: 7,548* read the crawling headline. Cary and Kayo walked around taking in the growing celebratory atmosphere. New figures were posted every few minutes. By nine o'clock, with nearly 20 percent of the vote counted, the "no" vote had surged to a 51.5 percent to 48.5 percent lead. The crowd became more excited, more electric. Forty percent of the vote had been counted by nine thirty. The "no" vote lead had grown to 52 percent. At ten, slightly more than 50 percent of the votes had been tallied with 53 percent of Columbiana's electorate voting "no."

Cary and Kayo mingled with other gay marriage supporters, coming face-to-face with Marletta Gaines and a man they assumed was her husband. They saw University of Columbiana Big Men on Campus Aaron Lanphere and Russell Kim. Cary literally bumped into Davis Wells as he was being interviewed by Kimberly Teller, causing Wells to spill some white wine on his Gucci loafers.

The incident was caught on camera, including Davis' momentary look of uncontrolled anger. As ten thirty approached, with 62 percent of the vote in, the lead had grown to 54 percent. On-air analysts and commentators began declaring Initiative 614's defeat. Even CNN mentioned it in its national election coverage. It appeared certain Columbiana had made history by approving gay marriage in a public vote.

Overheated by the crowded hall and excitement, Cary and Kayo decided to step outside, onto the front porch of the stately mansion to cool off. They sidestepped embracing couples of every gender combination. They passed between celebrants who clearly had had too much to drink. They slipped around individuals crying with happiness. One of them was a man in his sixties wearing red silk pajamas. He was being held by a man in white shorts and a white shirt with red suspenders and tennis shoes with red laces. Cary stopped to observe the touching, emotional moment. Kayo looked the duo over and said, "Cool outfits." The men did not hear the compliment. Instead, the man in white pulled away from his partner and looked him in the eye. "We can get married!" he said with excitement, stressing the final word. Then he said it again, emphasizing the first word.

Cary and Kayo dodged people craning their necks trying to find television screens to watch and they passed people staring off in shocked disbelief. As they reached the entry, they came upon a couple of inappropriately dressed young men. One wore a red velvet tuxedo with no shirt, exposing a well-defined chest. The other exuded ethnic mystery and startling handsomeness. He was wearing red Levis and a bowtie. He also had no shirt and he was barefoot. They looked like models on a photo shoot. As Cary and Kayo neared the men, Cary heard the Levi-clad one celebrate, "Oh my god, Shawn, we won! I don't believe it. Shawn, it's really true. We won!"

When Cary and Kayo reached the front porch, they realized they had not been the only ones needing to cool down in the fresh air. They stepped between several people fanning themselves. They stepped around several people smoking. They even smelled a hint of marijuana. They stepped down to the first step, next to the sidewalk, where no one else stood. Cars driving past the mansion honked. Passengers in the vehicles cheered. Cary turned back and looked at the mansion. The large "No on I-614" banner wafted happily in the wind.

Cary turned to Kayo. "This is unbelievable," he said. "Who would have ever guessed you and I would find each other after all these years, get together, and take up where we left off? Only this time, we won the war!"

"Yes, we did, man. Yes, we did," Kayo agreed. They started laughing, giggling actually, innocent childlike sounds of pure joy, pure happiness. They embraced for a long, lingering moment, patting each other's backs. As they pulled apart, Cary noticed a black car slowly approach the load zone in front of them and pull in. Cary saw something that puzzled him. "Why does that car have a Russian license plate?" he asked.

Kayo turned and looked at the car. "It says 'Mir' on the side," he noted. "'Mir' means 'peace.'"

"I know," Cary responded as the driver of the car rolled down his window. The driver looked out.

"Hi, Dad," he said.

"Nick!" Cary shouted, stunned by the unexpected appearance of his estranged son. As he blurted, "What are you doing here?" the passenger side door opened. Out stepped a young man. He walked around the front of the car and faced Kayo. It was Andrei Smirnov.

"Andrei?" Kayo asked, confusion lacing his voice.

In a quick, unexpected move, Smirnov threw a powerful punch landing directly on Kayo's jaw. Kayo crumbled immediately, falling backward and hitting his head squarely on a marble step behind him. Blood began pouring out of his left ear. Brains oozed out of the back of his head.

Cary screamed Kayo's name. He screamed it again. He turned toward the mansion and screamed, "Help!" But no one was there. No political banner danced in the breeze across the majestic house's face. He turned toward the mysterious black car and his son. But they were not there. The street, teaming with activity moments before, was empty. The surrounding silence roared in Cary's head. He turned and bent over his longtime friend, helplessly, frantically calling his name.

"Kayo! Kayo! Oh, my god, Kayo!"

FRIDAY, FEBRUARY 4, 2011

Panicked, startled, breathless, Cary suddenly awoke in his gray Lazy-Boy recliner. He bolted upright. He was still wearing his navy blue North Face winter coat. *Columbiana City's Number One News Source--KEHT Channel 8--February 4, 2011* crawled across the television screen in front of him.

"Oh, my god. Oh, Kayo," he panted. "That was all a dream!" he realized as he returned to reality. Then he corrected himself. *Hell,* he thought, *that was no dream. That was a fucking nightmare. Just like the decades-long nightmare gays and lesbians have experienced fighting for equal rights. They've had to listen to the lies and hear the name-calling. They've endured violence and pain. They've tasted political victories just to have them challenged, even repealed.* Cary swallowed. He began to shake, a post-trauma shiver. He grasped the recliner's arm rests to steady himself. *Maybe that nightmare, just like mine, is over.* He rubbed his eyes and closed them for a moment. His trembling ceased. I flicker of a smile appeared. *Thank God! None of that happened. That campaign didn't happen. None of those deaths were real. I didn't kill anyone. Kayo didn't kill anyone,* Cary thought as total relief swept through his body. *We didn't cross that line, that line we swore we wouldn't cross in the '70s. We swore we wouldn't commit violence against people, no matter what they said or did, no matter how much we hated what they stood for. And we didn't. It was not acceptable then. It isn't acceptable now. Thank God, we didn't really become people like that. We didn't become terrorists. If all that had been true, we would have been terrorists, smalltime terrorists, but terrorists just the same.*

A ripple of a satisfied smile sneaked onto Cary's face. He opened his eyes, smiled more broadly, and pounded the recliner's arm in celebration. But his expression quickly became serious again. *Why did we ever think violence against things or organizations was different?* he thought. *Why did we think that was acceptable? Because we were young, idealistic, and full of...* Cary looked around the reality of his living room. *Oh, shit. That means I still haven't found you, man. I still haven't found you, Kayo. I still don't know what ever happened to you. And I still feel guilty.*

Cary stared with glassy eyes at the television for a moment and then clicked the set into silence. He rose from the chair, took off his coat and hung it on its hook by the front door, ambled into the kitchen, and prepped his coffeemaker. He sat at his kitchen table gazing unfocused at its wood grain while he waited for the gurgling and dripping to end. His jumbled thoughts bounced from events in his dream to events in his life. The common denominator in them all was Kayo, the vision of his face or the sound of his name. The coffeemaker stopped dripping. Cary didn't notice.

He wandered into his bedroom and fell prone on his bed. He grabbed one of his pillows, pulled it to him, and hugged it, burying his face in its yellow pillowcase. *All I want to know is that you're OK,* he pleaded. *And that you forgive me.* Then, without warning, he erupted in uncontrolled sobs. His tears soaked the pillow with pain, regret, and loneliness. Cary had not cried like this since Lisa died.

He wept for fifteen minutes and then fell asleep, exhausted by the breaching of his emotional dam. Cary awoke at eleven o'clock and struggled to get up, but only managed to reach the edge of the bed, where he sat, hands on his knees, staring at the floor. After several minutes, his gaze focused on his pant legs. *Shit,* he thought, *I'm still wearing yesterday's clothes.*

Cary bolted upright, undressed and dashed to the bathroom. He stood in his shower longer than usual, hoping the hot water would rid him of any remnants of his traumatic night in the recliner. He shaved quickly, dressed, and poured a cup of his hours-old coffee. He toasted two bagels, spreading peanut butter on one and cream cheese on the other, and sat down at his kitchen table. By the time Cary finished the bagels and coffee, it was time for KEHT's noon news. He returned to the bathroom to brush his teeth before heading to the living room. This last stop, however, caused him to miss the first minutes of the newscast.

Cary simultaneously clicked the remote and sat down on the edge of his recliner. As the picture appeared on the screen, a vaguely familiar face stared at him. Cary instantly saw the name superimposed below it: Kirk Alexander.

"Seventies anti-war activist Kirk Alexander returns to Columbiana City," Lacey Powers was saying, "after a decades-long self-exile in Toronto. He will take a leadership role in the local chapter of the national civil rights organization One Nation in Equality."

"Oh, my god," Cary gasped. *You're back and you're Kirk now. Kirk. Not Kayo. No wonder I couldn't find you,* he thought. He fell back in his chair, his heart pounding as if he had just won the lottery. He studied the face on the screen, the older Kayo, now Kirk. *Where's your ponytail, man? You don't have your fucking ponytail.*

"Alexander brings with him," Lacey continued, "his partner of thirty years: Canadian native, former Columbiana City resident, and retired member of Canadian parliament, Ben Lieber."

"What!" Cary shouted. He stared at the television, no longer aware of its sounds or images. His eyes misted with joy, his heart pounded like an ecstatic bass drum, and the cilia in his ears vibrated, ever so slightly, to a mysterious, distant stimulus. Slowly, it came closer, grew louder, and became recognizable. Cary could hear a familiar laugh, a laugh that combined jolly with sinister. His soul danced.

A moment passed. An unexpected thought, a second reality, embraced Cary, wrapping him in added warmth. *Hey, now Kayo and I actually can work together to defeat the Al Kirks of the world. And we can do it in a civil manner! We could end a real life nightmare and, if statewide voters affirm equal rights for gays and lesbians, turn it into a dream come true. If not this year, maybe next year.* He gazed toward the living room window in blissful disbelief. Sunlight peeked into the living room. It bathed the room in dreamy light. It smiled warm, golden rays of hope on Cary. It lit the way into a bright future.